"I don't like you, mister . . . "

". . . How 'bout you just empty your pockets?"

"I told you to let it be," Win warned.

"Let it be? I'll show you how to let it be," the gunman said. Swinging his pistol toward Win, he thumbed back the hammer, but that was as far as he got. Win pulled the trigger on his own gun. His slug caught the would-be robber in the chest, and the robber, shocked by the sudden turn of events, dropped his own gun then put his hand over the wound, trying to stem the quick flow of blood.

BUSHWHACKERS
THE DYING TOWN

B. J. Lanagan

JOVE BOOKS, NEW YORK

THE DYING TOWN

A Jove Book / published by arrangement with
the author

PRINTING HISTORY
Jove edition / February 1998

The Putnam Berkley World Wide Web site address is
http://www.berkley.com

ISBN: 0-515-12232-7

A JOVE BOOK®
Jove Books are published by The Berkley Publishing Group,
a member of Penguin Putnam Inc.,
200 Madison Avenue, New York, New York 10016.
JOVE and the "J" design are trademarks belonging to Jove
Publications, Inc.

PRINTED IN THE UNITED STATES OF AMERICA

10 9 8 7 6 5 4 3 2 1

1

THE AFTERNOON TRANQUILLITY WAS BROKEN BY TWO MEN riding at a gallop down the middle of Main Street. They whooped and shouted and fired their pistols in the air, and the long-suffering citizens of Belle Springs could do nothing but shiver in fear and resignation. They pulled back even deeper into the homes and businesses where they were taking refuge.

From the second floor of Jackson's Hardware Store, Clem Beale, the barber, pulled the window shade to one side and looked down at the two riders.

"What is it?" someone asked. "What's going on?"

"Nothing, really. Just a couple of the sheriff's deputies having a little *fun*," Beale answered, accenting the word fun. "It's Deputies Reeves and Cummins. They're just shooting into the air."

"Even just shooting into the air is dangerous enough," Bob Deneke said. "A couple of weeks ago I had to replace a window in front of my feed store because one of the deputies got drunk and began shooting wildly."

"Be glad it was just a windowpane," one of the others said.

"Yes, you're right. What if my wife or one of my children had been in front of the store?"

"Seems to me like the very least we could expect is for a body ought to be safe in his own house or place of business," Arnold Jackson said.

"It's strange, isn't it, that we are being terrorized by the very people who are supposed to protect us?" Ed Randol asked. Randol was editor of the town newspaper. "I'm tellin' you men, we've got to do something about it."

Beale let the shade fall back in place, then returned to his chair to rejoin the others. This was an impromptu town meeting of most of the merchants and businessmen of the town. The meeting had been suggested by Ed Randol as a way of discussing what they could do to ease the situation in a town that was being run in a roughshod fashion by a sheriff who had declared Belle Springs an "open town." Arnold Jackson had opened the front part of the upstairs of his hardware store for the meeting. The back half of the second floor of the hardware store was occupied by Doc Boyer's office. Doc Boyer was also present.

"Perhaps we should do nothing," Parson Rockwall suggested. Ostensibly Methodist, Parson Rockwall was aware of his position as the only Protestant minister in town, and thus accommodated an ecumenical congregation, even offering to dunk those who preferred an immersion type baptism. There was also a Roman Catholic church, over on Third Street, on the other side of the railroad tracks, but its priest, Father Gomez, tended to a flock that was mostly Mexican, and neither the padre nor any of his parish were present for the meeting.

"What do you mean we could do nothing, Parson?" Luther Semmes, the owner of the leather goods store, asked. "By God, we've tried doing nothing, and it hasn't worked. Excuse my language."

"No, we haven't done nothing," the parson said. "I mean, we haven't actively done nothing."

"Parson, what in the Sam Hill are you talking about?"

"Think about it for a moment, gentlemen. Why does anyone come to a town like this in the first place?" Parson

Rockwall asked. "They come to town for the goods and services a town can provide: food, clothing, saddles, guns and ammunition, beer, whiskey, haircuts . . . everything that civilization offers. Now, suppose we didn't offer anything here? Suppose we got every merchant to shut down his business?"

"For how long?"

"For as long as it takes," the parson answered. "When the sheriff and his deputies can no longer take advantage of the things a town has to offer . . . when they can no longer collect a 'sheriff's tax' because no business is being done . . . why, perhaps they'll leave our town and go somewhere else."

"In other words, make Sheriff Pendrake be someone else's worry?" Jackson asked.

"Well, yes, in a manner of speaking," the parson admitted.

"And what about the townspeople during that time?" Dan Dunnigan asked. Dunnigan was proprietor of the general store. "I've got folks who depend on me. What are they supposed to do for food and clothing?"

"Yeah, and what about the rest of us merchants?" Semmes asked. "How are we supposed to make a living?"

"I didn't say it would be easy," Parson Rockwall replied. "I just said it was a possibility, something we might consider."

"Parson, I can't even begin to consider your recommendation," Doc Boyer said. "I've got a couple of women who are expecting children. Now, I know babies have been coming into this world long before there were doctors, but it looks like Mrs. Mapelby is going to have a difficult birth. What if she starts to deliver? Am I supposed to just stand by and do nothing?"

"Well, no, of course not," the parson stammered. "I mean, I wouldn't expect you to just let someone die."

"Speaking of dying," Parker Luscomb, the undertaker, put in. "Suppose someone does die during this period. Am I to leave them unburied?"

"Well, no," the parson admitted.

"And what about church on Sunday? Will you suspend it as well?"

"I wouldn't think so," the parson replied. "I mean, I would think that people would need God more than ever under such circumstances, wouldn't you?"

"All right, so how effective can we be, Parson?" Deneke asked. He began counting off the exceptions on his fingers. "Doc will be working, the undertaker will still be working, you'll still be working, and, like Dunnigan says, people will still need food. Besides that, the sheriff owns the Gilded Cage saloon, so you know it isn't going to be shut down. And Lem Quartermouse owns the Desert Flower, but he's out of town right now, and you know Harry Conners won't shut it down without Quartermouse tells him to. So where does that leave us?"

"That pretty much leaves us with no plan," Randol said.

"Then, what are we going to do?" Beale asked.

"What if we fight fire with fire?" Jackson suggested.

"What do you mean?"

"What if we could get someone to oppose Sheriff Pendrake?"

"Oppose him? You mean run against him in an election?" Deneke asked.

"No, that wouldn't do any good," Jackson said. "Pendrake isn't going to let us have an election."

"Then, oppose him in what way?" Deneke asked.

"I mean find someone who will stand up to the sheriff and his deputies and do what it takes to clean up the town."

"Do what it takes?"

"Yes."

"You are just beating around the bush here, Jackson," Randol said. "Tell us exactly what you mean."

"I think he means kill the sheriff," Deneke said. He looked at Jackson. "That is what you mean, isn't it, Jackson?"

Jackson was silent for a moment, then he took a deep breath and let it out audibly. "Actually, I would prefer that Pendrake leave of his own accord if he is confronted. But if the only way we can get rid of him is to kill him, then, yes, that's what I mean,'' he finally said.

"Who do you propose to do that?'' Deneke asked. "One of us?''

Jackson shook his head. "No,'' he said. "We aren't killers.''

"Then who?''

"I don't know. Maybe we can find someone.''

"You mean hire someone?''

"If necessary.''

"To kill the sheriff? You are suggesting that we hire a killer?''

Jackson looked squarely at Deneke, then, without blinking an eye, said, "Yes. If we have to go out and hire a killer, then I think that is what we should do.''

"God in heaven, listen to you men!'' the parson gasped. "You are not only talking about murder, you are talking about doing it in such a way that the entire town will be involved.''

"We're not talkin' about murder,'' Beale said. "We're talkin' about standin' up for our rights.''

"No, you aren't. You are talking about getting someone in here to commit murder. Gentlemen, I must tell you that a sin of that magnitude . . . the sin of murder . . . is not one that decreases as you increase the number of participants. Indeed, it is venal enough to corrupt all. If we do murder, gentlemen, it will make us no better than the men we are trying to eliminate,'' the parson said. "Can't you men see that?''

"Yeah, well, Preacher, sometimes there just ain't no other way,'' Jackson said. "Not too many years back, you might recollect, this whole country was pushed into violence. We fought us one hell of a war, North and South. I was just a young man from Illinois then, but I picked up a gun and I went to war. And believe me, I seen enough killin' and dyin' at Antietam to last me a lifetime. But I didn't go through all that just so's I could come out west and kowtow to a bunch of varmints like Sheriff Pendrake and his deputies. No, sir, if somebody was to happen to kill that son of a bitch, as far as I'm concerned, he'd have my support.''

Rockwall picked up his small, low-crown parson's hat and put it on his head.

''Gentlemen, I can't, in all good conscience, stay here while such a conversation is taking place. I will make no further effort to stop you, but neither can I actively support you. If you'll excuse me, I'll just be on my way.''

''I'm real sorry you feel that way, Parson Rockwall,'' Jackson said. ''I think that now, more than any other time, a town needs the moral guidance of a preacher.''

''Moral guidance?'' Parson Rockwall repeated. He sighed and shook his head. ''God help me, I thought that was exactly what I just trying to do for you. Good day, gentlemen.''

The others watched Rockwall go down the stairs, then they heard the door down on the street open and shut.

''Ah, the hell with him. We don't need him anyway,'' Jackson said.

''Actually, we do. It would have been good to have him on our side. His support would have lent a degree of moral credence to what we are plannin' to do. It would have gone a long way toward gettin' rid of any squeamishness some of the townspeople might have against killing the sheriff.''

''Yes, well, no matter how you sugarcoat it, there's always goin' to be someone who'll call it by its name. The parson is right, it's murder, gentlemen. But, by God, I'm beginnin' to feel like it's the only thing left for us.''

ACROSS THE STREET FROM THE HARDWARE STORE, THE two deputies who had been discharging their weapons in the middle of the street a few minutes earlier were now inside the Gilded Cage saloon. Deputy Reeves, drinking whiskey from a bottle, walked over to look out across the top of the batwing doors onto the street. He turned the bottle up for a long, Adam's-apple-bobbing drink, then he pulled the bottle down and wiped his mouth with the back of his hand.

''Hey, Cummins, come over here and look at this,''

Reeves said, laughing. "This is about the funniest lookin' thing I ever seen."

Cummins, who was also drinking his whiskey straight from the bottle, was leaning against the bar.

"What you see that's so funny, Reeves?" he asked.

"The hat Parson Rockwall is wearing. Come over here and take a gander at it."

Cummins walked over to the batwing doors. "What about it?" he asked.

"What about it? Hell, you blind? It's right there," Reeves said. "Look at the crown of that hat. Look how low down it is. Why, I bet it ain't no more'n two inches from the top of the head. And now, look how wide the brim is. Plus, it's got them two little black ribbons hangin' down the back. The fella that made that hat musta been drunk or somethin'."

Cummins took a drink of his whiskey, then lowered the bottle. "Don't see nothin' all that funny about it. That's the kind of hat all preachers wear, far as I know."

"The hell you say?" Reeves examined the hat through eyes that seemed to be swimming in their sockets. "Bet I could shoot it off his head," he added.

"From how far?"

"From here."

Cummins measured the distance between the door of the saloon and the approaching preacher.

"The hell you say," he said. "That crown's pretty low, and he's a good hunnert and fifty feet away."

"It'd be a hell of a shot, I admit that. But I got me ten bucks says I can do it," Reeves insisted, taking out his pistol. "I'm just goin' to let him get a little closer."

"All right, I'll take that bet. But you see the other end of that water trough?" Cummins pointed it out.

"Yeah, I see it. What about it?"

"That's too close. If you don't shoot the hat off before he gets there, the bet's off."

"Get your ten bucks ready," Reeves said, taking careful aim.

•   •   •

BACK ON THE SECOND FLOOR OF JACKSON'S HARDWARE
store, Bob Deneke, feeling a need to stretch his legs, had
gotten up and moved over to the window. He was watching
the preacher walk down the street. Behind him he could
hear the buzz of conversation as the businessmen of the
town continued to discuss the few options they had, with
regard to how best they might handle the sheriff.

Suddenly Deneke saw a flash of light and a puff of
smoke emerge from just inside the saloon door. A second
later he heard the shot and at almost the same time he saw
the preacher pitch backward. Rockwall fell on his back with
his arms stretched out in the dirt on either side of him. His
hat rolled off into the street, and his head was tilted back.
Clearly visible, even from the second floor of the hardware
store, was the large, bloody hole in the middle of Rockwall's forehead.

"Oh, my God!" Deneke gasped.

The others looked toward him.

"What is it, Bob? What'd you just see?"

"They just shot the preacher," Deneke said in a quiet,
tight voice.

"What?" Beale asked. He rushed over to the window,
followed by the others.

"My God, who did it?"

"I don't know, exactly," Deneke said. "But I seen the
puff of smoke. The shot come from the Gilded Cage."

Doc Boyer started quickly down the stairs.

"Doc, where you goin'?"

"To see if I can do anything for the preacher," the doctor called back over his shoulder.

The others, galvanized into action by Doc Boyer's quick
response, clomped rapidly and noisily down the stairs after
him, then ran out into the street. By the time they reached
Rockwall, there were already a couple of dozen people
gathered around the preacher's prostrate form. The way
Rockwall was lying, with his arms spread straight out to
either side of him, reminded Deneke of Christ on the cross,
though he didn't comment on it, for fear of someone taking
affront for it being sacrilegious.

"Can you do anything for him, Doc?" Jackson asked.

Doc Boyer squatted down beside the body, then sighed and shook his head. "I'm afraid not. He was dead before he hit the ground," he said, raising up again. He looked around. "What the hell happened? Who shot him, and why?"

"I reckon I done it," Reeves said. He had been standing back with the others.

"You did it? You're a deputy. You are supposed to uphold the law," Doc said. "What possible reason could you have had?"

"Now, see here, Doc, I didn't do it of a pure purpose. It was an accident," Reeves said.

"An accident, you say? Would you mind telling me just how in the hell you can accidentally shoot someone right between the eyes?"

"I bet ten dollars with Deputy Cummins, here, that I could shoot that funny little hat off the preacher's head," Reeves said. "I reckon I missed. I don't understand it, neither. I had me a real good bead on it. The preacher must of hopped up or somethin'."

"You bet ten dollars?" Doc Boyer said angrily. "You took a man's life for ten dollars?"

"Take it easy, Doc," a new voice said. "You heard my deputy say it was an accident."

When Doc Boyer looked toward the new speaker, he saw Sheriff Harley Pendrake just arriving on the scene. "Deputy Reeves, that was mighty careless of you," Pendrake continued.

"Yeah," Reeves agreed, hanging his head contritely. "I'm real sorry 'bout that. Hell, I didn't have nothin' against the preacher. Far as I knew, he was a real nice fella."

"What are you goin' to do about it, Sheriff?" Deneke asked. "I mean you can't just treat this as if nothing has happened."

Pendrake exhaled audibly. "You're right. Reeves, Cummins, you're going to have to pay for this."

"Now, hold on here, Sheriff," Reeves said. "I done told

you it was an accident. And I'm just real goddamned sorry for it. And I told these here folks how remorseful I am. Seems to me that ought to be the end of it."

"Yeah, well, bein' sorry ain't quite enough," Pendrake said. "What was it you said you bet? Ten dollars?"

"Yeah, ten dollars."

"All right, that would make the pot total twenty dollars. I'll take that twenty dollars."

"Hold on, Sheriff," Cummins said. "That ain't hardly right. The money's rightfully mine now. I won the bet. Besides which, I didn't shoot the son of a bitch, Reeves did. And the way you're doin' it now, why, it's like Reeves ain't payin' nothin' a'tall, specially as how he already lost the money."

"You didn't shoot him but you . . . what's that word?" Pendrake asked. Then he smiled. "Oh, yeah, you aided and abetted. But you're right, Reeves needs to pay more, so I'll take twenty dollars from each of you."

"Wait a minute, that means I'm out a total of thirty dollars here," Reeves complained.

"Pay up," Pendrake ordered.

Grumbling, the two men handed over the money. "It don't seem right to me," Reeves said. "Hell, I told you it was an accident."

"Accident or not, the preacher's dead and he's goin' to need a decent buryin'," Pendrake said. He took the money from his two deputies, then gave it to Luscomb. "Undertaker, you see to it he gets buried good and proper," he said.

"I ain't chargin' nothin' for the buryin'," Luscomb said. "I'll give this money to the preacher's church."

"I'm sure the preacher would like that," Pendrake said. "Come on, boys," he added, speaking to his deputies. "Let's get a drink and let these folks bury their preacher in peace."

"Jackson," Deneke said as Pendrake and his deputies walked back across the street toward the Gilded Cage. "You're right. Somebody has got to take care of that son of a bitch."

"I agree," Beale said. "But who?"

"You know," Randol said, "I'm not really much of a religious man. But the preacher getting killed like that?" He shook his head. "I don't believe we're goin' to have to find anybody. I've got me a feeling that the Lord has already put things in motion to set things right again."

2

ON THE EVENING OF THAT SAME DAY, RACING TOWARD the brilliant scarlet and gold sunset beneath the darkening vaulted sky, the *Southwest Flyer* thundered across the mesquite-dotted landscape. Inside the Baldwin 4-4-0 locomotive, the engineer held the throttle wide open while his fireman threw chunks of wood into the roaring flames of the firebox. The train was exactly on schedule, whipping past a milepost every one hundred and twenty seconds.

Behind the engine and the tender was a string of coach cars, and, inside these, the travelers were getting down to the business of eating their supper. As there was no dining car, the passenger cars were filled with the smells of dried beef, hot peppers, spicy sausages, and smoked cheeses from the boxed lunches the passengers had brought on board with them.

Win Coulter was sitting in the last seat on the left side of the car. His legs were pulled up so that his knees rested on the seat back in front of him, and his hat was tilted down over his eyes. Unlike the others, he had no boxed lunch. He had eaten a piece of jerky at about three in the afternoon, and that would have to do, for now.

Win was going to Belle Springs, where he would meet
his brother Joe. During the late war Win and Joe had ridden
with Quantrill and Bloody Bill Anderson. They were called
Bushwhackers then, and though the name was meant to be
derogatory, it was an appellation they now accepted with
pride. The only survivors of their family, the two brothers
generally ran together. But three weeks ago Joe had accepted a job taking some horses to a ranch in West Texas.
At the time, Win happened to be riding a winning streak
in one of the local saloons, so he opted to stay on for a
while.

Then, yesterday, a man named Lem Quartermouse drew
a full house of aces and kings. To cover his bet he put forth
a deed for the Desert Flower, an establishment he claimed
was the finest saloon in Belle Springs.

Win was holding three queens, and when he drew the
fourth, Quartermouse sighed, then pushed the deed across
the table.

"You won it, Coulter, fair and square," he said.

"Would you like to buy it back?" Win asked. "I won't
hold you up."

Quartermouse paused for a moment. "No," he said.
"No, I don't think I do want to buy it back. It's a good
saloon, Mr. Coulter, and there are some good people working there. They deserve something better than the best I can
do for 'em. You may be the best thing that ever happened
to them."

Owning a saloon had never been in Win's plans, but now
that he had drawn the hand, he decided he would play the
cards. He sent a telegram to Joe suggesting that, instead of
coming back here, they should meet in Belle Springs. That
was where he was headed now.

As he sat in his seat, rocked by the gentle rhythm of the
train, he gradually slipped off to sleep. He had been sleeping for about an hour when the train suddenly ground to a
shuddering, screeching, banging halt.

Win woke with a start.

"What is it?" someone asked.

"I don't know. The train is stopping, for some reason," another answered.

"Well, if we are going to stop at every rock and cactus in the entire Southwest, the management of this railroad will certainly hear from me," the first man said. "This is no way to run a business."

Win looked through the window. It was very dark outside, but he did see several horses, shadows moving through the blackness. He knew instantly what was going on, so he pulled his pistol from his holster and let it rest on his knee, covering it with his hat.

Suddenly someone burst into the car from the front. He was wearing a bandanna tied across the bottom half of his face. He was also holding a pistol, which he waved toward the passengers in the car.

"Everyone stay in their seats!" the masked man shouted.

"See here! What is the meaning of this? What is going on?" a man shouted indignantly. "I have already stated my intention of reporting this to the railroad, and this unseemly behavior will come in for special attention!"

He started to get up from his seat, but the gunman moved quickly toward him and brought his pistol down sharply over the man's head. The passenger groaned and fell back. The woman who was with him cried out in alarm.

"Report it to the railroad? You damned fool, we're robbin' this here railroad!" the gunman said gruffly. "Now, ever'one stay in their seats like I said! The next man that stands up, I aim to shoot."

Another gunman came into the car to join the first.

"Any trouble in here?" he asked.

"Nothin' I can't handle myself. What's goin' on outside?"

"Ever'thing is goin' like it's supposed to, Billy. Loomis is coverin' the engineer, and Beatie is robbin' the mail car."

"Damn you, Deekus! What the hell's the purpose for wearin' these masks, if you're goin' to call ever'one by name?"

"You're right. I wasn't thinkin'," Deekus said.

"That's 'cause you got no brains to think with. Now, get on back to the next car and keep ever'one in their seats."

"How will I know when the rest of you leave?"

"Just keep your eyes open, that's all. Now, get on back there."

As the second gunman started down the aisle toward the next car, he looked over toward Win, then stopped.

"Mister, I don't like the way you're lookin' at me," the gunman said.

"Let it be, friend," Win said. "Just go on about your business."

"Haw!" The gunman laughed out loud. He turned toward the other robber. "Hey, Billy, d'you hear what this fella said? He tol' me to jus' go on about my business."

"Will you shut your mouth, you damn fool," Billy said.

Flustered because he had fouled up again, the gunman turned back to Win.

"I don't like you, mister. How 'bout you just empty your pockets?"

"I told you to let it be," Win warned.

"Let it be? I'll show you how to let it be," the gunman said. Swinging his pistol toward Win, he thumbed back the hammer, but that was as far as he got. Win pulled the trigger on his own gun, and a finger of fire stabbed through his hat. His slug caught the would-be robber in the chest, and the robber, shocked by the sudden turn of events, dropped his own gun then put his hand over his wound, trying to stem the quick flow of blood.

"What the hell?" Billy shouted from the front of the car. He fired and his bullet crashed through the glass beside Win, cutting his face with sharp shards of glass. The others in the car screamed and got down, as Win returned fire. Billy staggered back, his hands to his throat, blood spilling through his fingers.

As the car filled with the gun smoke of the three discharges, Win got out of his seat and scooted out through the back door of the car. He jumped from the steps down to the ground, then fell and rolled off into the darkness.

"Billy, Deekus! What's goin' on in there?" someone called. "What's goin' on?"

In the dim light that spilled through the car windows, Win saw the gunman who was yelling at the others. This was Loomis, who had been covering the engineer, and now he was moving quickly toward the back of the train. As he ran through the little golden patches of light it had the effect of a lantern show, blinking on and off so that first he was in shadow, then illuminated, then in shadow, then illuminated.

Win raised his pistol and pointed toward the next window, waiting for Loomis to pass through the light. But Loomis had suddenly realized what he was doing, and he remained in the shadow.

"Loomis!" a voice called from the darkness. "Loomis, we got to get!"

"Somethin's happened to Billy and Deekus!" Loomis called back.

"That's their problem! We got to get!"

"Billy is my brother!" Loomis shouted. "I ain't leavin' my brother!"

"Have it your own way," the voice called from the darkness. "I'm gettin' out!"

Win heard horse's hooves as a rider hurried off into the darkness.

"Beatie! Beatie, you come back here, you son of a bitch!"

Loomis began firing in the darkness, his bullets flying toward the galloping horse. Each time he fired, the two-foot wide flame pattern lit him up as brightly as a photographer's flash powder.

"Drop your gun, Loomis," Win said. "I've got a bead on you."

Loomis suddenly spun and started firing toward the sound of Win's voice. He was firing blindly, but his bullets were coming frighteningly close, because Win could hear them whistling by.

Win returned fire, and Loomis let out a little yell, then fell.

Win moved through the darkness toward him, then knelt alongside.

"Why didn't you leave when you had the chance?" he asked.

"You got a brother, mister?" Loomis asked in a pained gasp.

"Yes."

"Then you ought not to have to ask that question. Me 'n Billy is all that's left. I couldn't leave him." He gasped a few more times, then his labored breathing stopped.

"You didn't leave him," Win said, straightening up and putting his gun away.

By now, with the shooting over, a few other brave souls were beginning to climb down from the train. Gradually they filled the space alongside the track, looking cautiously out into the darkness as they moved toward Win and the body that lay on the ground beside him.

"Is he dead?" one of the passengers asked.

"Yes," Win said.

"So's them two inside."

The engineer and the conductor appeared from the darkness.

"They get anything off any of the passengers?" the conductor asked.

"Not a penny, thanks to this man," someone said, nodding toward Win.

"You shoulda seen him!" another said. "He took on all three of 'em, all by hisself."

"Mister, you're a genuine hero," the conductor said. "It's just too bad you weren't ridin' in the mail car."

"They get any money from there?" a passenger asked.

"I'll say they did. They got twelve hundred dollars," the conductor replied.

Someone whistled softly. "That's a good day's work."

"Yeah, especially when you figure it's all for one man," the engineer said.

"What do you mean, for one man?"

"Well, they was four of 'em stopped the train," the engineer said. "But when it was all over with, only one of 'em got away. He had the money and he's got no one to share it with."

"What are you goin' to do with the bodies?" one of the passengers asked.

"I don't know. I haven't really thought about it," the conductor replied.

"You can't leave 'em here."

"There's two dead in our car," another said. "Don't think I like that either."

"Get 'em into the baggage car," the conductor suggested. "We'll take 'em into Belle Springs and give 'em to the sheriff."

THE TOWN OF BELLE SPRINGS HAD BEGUN AS A MINING community. For more than two years, the Associated Mining Company of Belle Springs took out as much silver from their digs as was being mined at any other place in the country. During this time, several enterprising citizens discovered that there was more than one way to mine silver. Some did it with a pick and shovel, others did it with cards, or liquor, or a pretty smile and a shapely pair of legs.

Then, most of the veins played out, and the amount of silver being mined dropped dramatically. Concurrent with the depletion of the silver, however, was a major discovery of copper.

Not everyone was upset with the playing out of the silver mines. Silver, like gold, attracted get-rich-quick people. Copper, on the other hand, tended to attract only the most assiduous miners . . . the mining engineers and the hard-working men who went down into the shafts. These were the steady, sober-minded men who tended to start families and build towns. Such industriousness attracted stores, banks, schools, and freight and stage lines. There were also a few ranches nearby to take advantage of the railroad that came into town, and it began to look as if Belle Springs would become a real, productive city, until a man named Harley Pendrake came into the picture.

Pendrake was a small, unattractive man, with a pock-marked face, a drooping black moustache, a hawklike nose, and narrow, obsidian eyes. It was, perhaps, that unattractiveness which made him an outcast from society. As a result he had developed absolutely no social skills. He did, however, have one skill which marked him as a man with whom others would have to reckon. Harley Pendrake was a gunman with so few moral compunctions about killing that he could take the life of another man as easily as he could step on a cockroach.

Pendrake came to Belle Springs when the mines were still producing silver. He had been hired by the mining company to provide security for the silver shipments. Some, who knew of Pendrake's spotted past—he had robbed a few banks and held up a stage or two—suggested that using him to guard the silver was like setting the fox to watch the hen coop. Others insisted that you must "set a thief to catch a thief" and saw no problem whatever with using Pendrake to guard the silver shipments.

After the silver played out, however, there was no longer a need to provide guards over the ore shipments. That was because it took so much copper to turn a profit that the freight wagon gave way to the railroad as the prime carrier. Thus, by the time Associated Mining completed its change-over from silver to copper, Pendrake and his men found themselves out of work.

But those who breathed a sigh of relief over that fact soon learned, to their dismay, that Pendrake had no intention of leaving Belle Springs. Instead, he bullied a few of the town's officials into appointing him as the town sheriff, and his men as deputies. Now, with badges on their vests, they moved along the boardwalks, or through the streets of the town, pushing any and all out of their way. They would sometimes go so far as to pistol-whip some poor soul who was too slow in avoiding them. There had even been a few killings, usually over a dispute in a card game, but always justified as "self-defense," or "killed while resisting arrest for card cheating." The climactic event had occurred earlier this same day, when two of Pendrake's deputies killed the preacher "accidentally" while acting upon a bet.

By now the situation had reached the point to where very few of the decent citizens of Belle Springs would dare venture out of their homes. That hurt the business of the town's merchants, and as the legitimate stores began closing, the town began dying.

Even as the town was dying, however, it flared brightly, as drinking, gambling, and whoring became its major industry. Also news of the "wide-open" town spread throughout the West so that it began to attract new residents. The new residents, however, were not the kind of people the original citizens of the town wanted, for they were nothing more than carbon copies of Pendrake and his men. As more hoodlums arrived, the number of those who were sucking out the life's blood of the town became disproportionate to the number of those whose industriousness supplied the life's blood of the town. And, like an animal being drained by leeches, the town was slowly, but inexorably, sinking to its knees.

3

WIN KNEW NOTHING OF THE KILLING OF THE PREACHER, or the town's history when, just after ten P.M., he stepped down onto the station platform in Belle Springs, Texas. Behind him the train, while still, wasn't quiet. As it would be proceeding farther west, the fireman kept up the steam, and the relief valve continued to open and close in great, heaving sighs. Overheated wheel bearings and gearboxes popped and snapped as the tortured metal cooled. From the platform around him there came a discordant chorus of squeals, laughter, shouts, and animated conversations as people were getting on and off the train.

Looking toward the baggage car, Win saw that the train robbers had been taken from the train and laid out, side by side. Already, a crowd was gathering around the bodies.

Win found their morbid curiosity somewhat unsettling. There had been more than one train robbery in his own checkered past, and he knew there might be more in the future. He could well imagine his brother Joe and himself in the same situation as these three men.

One of the curious train passengers reached down to untie the kerchief from the neck of one of the dead outlaws.

"Hold on there, mister! Just what do you think you are doing?" someone asked.

"Takin' this here fella's kerchief," the curious passenger answered. "I aim to have me a souvenir."

"Leave it alone."

"Who the hell says so?"

"I say so," an authoritative voice replied. "I am Sheriff Harley Pendrake, and if you try and take that kerchief, or anything else off any of these men, I'll throw you in jail."

Win looked toward Pendrake and saw a pock-faced man with a drooping moustache coming down the platform. Although he was a small man, there was the look of danger about him, and as he moved toward the bodies the assembled crowd parted before him, like the sea opening before Moses.

Pendrake wore his gun low on the right side. A five-pointed star, pinned to a leather vest, glinted in the light of the several flickering torches which illuminated the station platform.

"Sure thing, Sheriff," the passenger said. "Whatever you say."

"There's only three of 'em?" Pendrake asked. "Where's the other one?"

"There's only three killed," the conductor said. "There was another, but he got away . . . with the money shipment," he added.

"You don't say?" The sheriff stroked his chin. "And how much money would that be?" he asked.

"About twelve hundred dollars," the conductor answered. "It was a species transfer to the local bank."

A photographer hurried up to join them, lugging his camera and equipment. He set up the tripod, then started arranging the bodies, folding their arms across their chests. As an added touch, he put guns in their hands.

For a moment, Win had a touch of déjà vu, then he remembered that, during the late war, his lieutenant, Bloody Bill Anderson, had been photographed in the same gruesome way, right after he was killed.

"You ought to get a picture of that fella over there,"

someone said, pointing out Win. "He's the one kilt these outlaws."

"You don't say? All by hisself?" the photographer asked.

"Yep."

Smiling obsequiously, the photographer started toward Win.

"Mister, perhaps you would like your picture taken with them?" he suggested. "I could make you a nice copy for, oh, a dollar."

"And then sell copies of them to the public?" Win replied. "No thanks."

"Just tryin' to be helpful is all," the photographer said. "Most folks would want recognition for what they done."

The sheriff looked toward Win. "That right, mister? You the one shot these three men?"

"I'm the one."

"What's your name?"

"Coulter."

"Don't reckon I've ever heard of you," Pendrake said.

"Just as well," Win replied. "It's not a good sign when sheriffs start learning a man's name before he ever comes to town." He tried to make a joke of it, but the sheriff was a humorless man.

"How is it that you shot these three, while you let the one with the money get away?"

"Wasn't my job to protect the bank's money, Sheriff," Win answered. He nodded toward the bodies. "Wasn't even my job to stop these fellas, and if they hadn't shot at me first, I wouldn't of shot them."

A sudden lightning flash of magnesium powder indicated that the photographer had started his work.

"You sayin' they shot first, but you still bested them?" the sheriff asked, the expression on his face and the tone of his voice suggesting that he didn't quite believe Win.

"That's what I'm sayin'," Win replied.

"Yes. Well, it is curious, though, don't you think?" the sheriff asked. "I mean, if you and the fella who got away had worked out some sort of deal, why, you'd both be settin' pretty now, wouldn't you? With only the two of you to share in the money.''

"Pendrake, you accusing me of being in on this?'' Win asked.

"No,'' Pendrake said. "Not exactly. But I am the sheriff here, and I am supposed to think on such things. It's my job.''

"You think on it all you want,'' Win said. "But don't be makin' any accusations you can't back up.''

"Ain't makin' none,'' the sheriff said. "But if I was, believe me, I could back them up. Just thought I'd let you know, though, that I aim to keep my eye on you for as long as you're in town.''

ALONG EITHER SIDE OF THE STREET LEADING INTO TOWN, false-fronted shanties competed for space. Subdued bubbles of soft light shone from the windows of the houses, while the saloons spilled a much brighter, golden light onto the boardwalks. The street was noisy with the cacophony of saloon patrons having a good time. From the nearest saloon came a man's hoarse guffaw, followed by a woman's high-pitched cackle. Someone broke a glass, and the crashing, tinkling sound enjoyed a moment of supremacy.

There were two saloons in town, and Win looked at both of them. One of them had a gilt-painted sign, reading: THE GILDED CAGE. The Gilded Cage, he also saw, was the center of all the noise and laughter, as it was doing a booming business.

The other saloon had no sign, and very little business. By the process of elimination he decided that this was the Desert Flower. Since this was the saloon he had won in a poker game, this was the one he headed for.

He pushed in through the batwing doors. To the left, as he entered, was a long bar. Towels hung on hooks about every five feet along its front. Behind the bar, a large mirror stretched the length of the wall. The paucity of customers in the place was reflected by the many empty tables Win saw in the mirror.

As he looked around, Win was somewhat surprised by

the lack of patrons, because with all the oak, glass, and gilt, this was obviously a very decent place. Why, then, was the Gilded Cage bursting at the seams with customers, while this place was practically empty? The question was much more than the mere curiosity of a customer. As he was the new owner, that was information he felt entitled to know. For the time being, however, he decided to keep to himself the fact that he was the new owner.

Win stepped up to the bar, and the bartender slid down toward him.

"We got whiskey and beer," the bartender said. "Which will it be?"

"What kind of whiskey?"

"Old Overholt. Two dollars the bottle, or ten cents the shot. Beer's five cents a glass."

"I'll have a beer."

The bartender pulled a glass down from a shelf in front of the mirror, then put it under the spigot and pulled the handle. Golden liquid slid up the inside of the glass then stopped at the top, where it was crowned by a foaming head.

"Thanks," Win said, taking the beer. He blew some of the foam off, then took a drink. The beer was good, so that couldn't be the cause of the lack of customers. Turning his back to the bar, he looked out over the saloon at the few who were patronizing the Desert Flower.

At the far end of the bar a young woman was drinking a beer. Her reddish-brown hair radiated in a wild array around her face, then cascaded down her back and across her shoulders. The dress she wore showed a generous amount of cleavage, and for a moment Win enjoyed the luxury of letting his eyes wander across her full breasts; flat, slender belly; and gently swelling hips. Smiling, he lifted his beer toward her. Lifting her own beer, she returned the smile.

"Would you care to have a drink with me, miss?" Win asked.

"Yes, I'd be glad to. Thank you," the woman replied, smiling as she moved down the bar to join him.

"One for the lady, barkeep."

"My name is Claire," the lady said. "And you are?"

"Coulter. Win Coulter."

The bartender put a drink in front of Claire, then slid a coin across the bar to Win.

"Your change, mister."

"Wait a minute," he said. "You're a little light, aren't you?"

"No, that's right."

"I believe you said beer was five cents?"

"That's right."

"I gave you a quarter, I bought two beers. I should get fifteen cents back. There's only a nickel here."

"A nickel each for the beers, and another nickel each for the sheriff's tax."

"The sheriff's tax? What the hell is the sheriff's tax?"

"If you want my opinion, it ain't a tax at all. It's downright stealin'," the bartender said.

"Harry, if I were you, I'd be careful about sharing my opinions," someone said. "You never know who's listening." The speaker, also standing at the bar, was an older, gray-haired man. He was rather well-dressed in a brown suit.

The bartender chuckled. "Now, that's real funny, hearin' such a thing from you, Doc, seein' as how you ain't never been none too shy 'bout sharin' your opinions with anyone."

"Well, that's different," Doc replied. "I'm an old man. Old people can get away with more things than young people can. Besides, I'm the only medical doctor within fifty miles, and the kind of town Pendrake runs generates a rather high demand for a doctor. He can't afford to lose me. On the other hand, bartenders are a dime a dozen. You, my friend, can be replaced in a heartbeat." The gray-haired man looked at Win, then stuck out his hand. "Ivan Boyer is the name, sir. But, as Harry said, I am a doctor, so most folks just call me Doc."

At that moment, a new patron pushed through the batwing doors and stepped into the saloon. Seeing Win, he stepped up to the bar.

"Say, you're the one that killed them outlaws, ain't you?" he asked.

"Yes," Win answered without elaboration.

"What outlaws?" Claire asked.

"Some outlaws tried to hold up the train tonight," the customer said. He pointed to Win. "This here fella killed three of 'em, and drove the fourth one off."

"You took on three men, all by yourself?" Claire asked, obviously impressed with the idea.

"Not willingly," Win replied. "What actually happened was they took me on. I didn't have much choice but to fight back."

"And kill all three of 'em," the recently arrived patron said. He chuckled. "I gotta tell you, mister, you've sure set the town to talkin'. Even Pendrake was impressed by what you done."

"You must be pretty good with a gun," Harry suggested. "Are you? Or were you just lucky?"

"A little of both, I guess," Win said modestly. "I was in the war. Folks get real familiar with guns during wartime."

"That's a fact, mister, it truly is," Harry replied. "I was in the war myself. Fifth Texas Artillery, it was. Who was you with?"

"I was with Quantrill," Win answered.

Harry's eyes grew big. "With Quantrill, you say? I've heard of him. It was a pretty nasty bunch of boys that rode with him."

There was a time in Win's life when he would have taken offense at Harry's remark. But it was an accurate remark, innocently stated, so Win just chuckled. "Well, we weren't Sunday School boys," he admitted.

"You goin' to be stayin' in town?" Harry asked.

"Yes, I figure on staying around for a while," Win replied.

"You plannin' on becomin' one of Pendrake's deputies?"

Win snorted what could have been a laugh. "Now, why would I want to do something like become a deputy?"

"Don't get me wrong. I'm certainly not recruiting for the sheriff," Doc replied. "But the truth is, being one of Pendrake's deputies is about the best job you can get in Belle Springs."

"Is that a fact? I never knew that deputies were so well paid," Win replied.

"I reckon they're not in most places," Harry said. "But Pendrake runs things a little different. He pays his deputies out of the tax he collects. And since he collects a lot of tax, he pays 'em well."

"And that's not all," Doc added. "In addition to the taxes Pendrake and his men collect, they also enjoy special reduced rates for the goods they buy from any of the merchants. Hell, they practically steal anything they want, and there's nothing we can do about it. We can't go to the law; they *are* the law!"

"They're bullies, all of them," Claire said bitterly. "They walk down the sidewalks, or through the streets of the town, just pushing people aside as if they owned the entire town."

"And the killings," Harry said. "Don't forget the killings."

"Yes," Doc put in. "There have been several killings, though they are always found innocent by reason of self-defense."

"Or like the killin' today," Harry said. He told about the preacher getting killed as a result of a bet between two drunk deputies as to whether or not one of them could shoot the hat off the preacher's head. "That one was ruled an accident."

"You mean Pendrake has the judge bullied as well?" Win asked.

Doc laughed bitterly. "Hell, Mr. Coulter, Pendrake *is* the judge," he said.

"Now, do you see how being a deputy can pay so well?" Harry asked.

"I see what you're sayin'," Win said. "But I have no

intention of working for him." He looked at Claire, smiling broadly. "The fact is, I'm going to work here, in the saloon."

"You're going to work here?" Claire asked, surprised by his statement. "Doing what?"

"Doing whatever I need to," Win answered. He still had not told them he was the new owner.

"Mr. Coulter, the fella that owns the place is out of town right now," Harry said, "and I can't speak for him. But even if he was here, I don't think he would hire you. It's not that he wouldn't want to, or even that you wouldn't be a good man to have around here. But he can't afford it. Hell, he's way behind in payin' me my wages. This place just isn't making any money."

Win looked around the saloon. "I noticed that there aren't many customers. Why is that? This seems like a decent enough place to me. You'd think a place like this would make lots of money."

"It used to make lots of money," Harry answered. "Why, there wasn't a saloon between here and San Antone that done better. But ever since the sheriff slapped on his tax, business has been way down."

"The saloon down the street seems to be doing all right," Win observed.

"I'll say it is," Harry replied. "We used to have two other bartenders in here, but they went down the street to work. Same thing with all the girls. Claire's the only one who stayed."

"And you stayed," Win said to Harry.

"Yes," Harry answered. "I might be crazy, but I stayed."

"Why?" Win asked. "I mean if you're making no money. Why did you stay?"

Harry continued to wipe glasses as he glanced around the saloon. "Barkeepin' ain't just a job for me," he said. "It's a profession. And a fella ought to practice his profession in a place he can be proud of. I couldn't work in the Gilded Cage. I don't want to work in a place where they water their whiskey and they cheat their customers."

"I feel the same way," Claire said. "I might be a soiled dove, but I do have some honor."

Win looked at Claire, then smiled. "Well, I don't know about the girls who left here to go over there," he said. "But without even looking, I believe I'd have to say that the Desert Flower got the best end of the bargain."

Claire returned his smile. "Why, thank you, sir," she said. "What a nice thing to say."

"It does make me curious, though," Win continued. "Why is the Gilded Cage doing so much better than the Desert Flower?"

"That's an easy enough question to answer," Harry said. "Folks who buy a drink in here have to pay the sheriff's tax. Folks who buy a drink at the Gilded Cage don't. That means they can drink twice as much, for the same amount of money."

"The Gilded Cage doesn't pay any taxes? Why is that?"

"Because Harley Pendrake owns it," Harry answered.

4

JOE'S COFFEEPOT WAS SUSPENDED OVER THE OPEN FLAMES, and the handle was so hot that he had to use his hat in order to pour himself a second cup of coffee. He was about to hang the pot up again when he sensed, rather than saw or heard, that someone was watching him. The hair on the back of his neck stood on end, and he forced himself to take a slow, deep breath, in order to remain calm.

"I got me nearly a whole pot of good coffee here if you're in the mind for some," he said easily.

There was a quiet chuckle from the dark, then Joe heard the sound of someone walking. A moment later a man appeared in the edge of the golden bubble of light cast from the small campfire.

"I guess I wasn't as quiet as I thought I was," the man said. He took a collapsible cup from his pocket and held it out. "Don't mind if I do," he added.

Joe poured the coffee and examined the man closely. The stranger had clear, blue eyes; a long, narrow face; and a bushy beard. Joe had never seen him before.

"That's kind of dangerous, isn't it?" Joe asked. "I mean, comin' up on a man's camp as quiet as all that."

The stranger took the cup, then squatted on his heels. He slurped a swallow of coffee through lips extended slightly to allow the coffee a chance to cool.

"I don't know, you might be right," the stranger admitted. "The truth is, I've never been able to figure out which way is best. Some folks are so nervous they'll just start banging away the moment they hear you, without even givin' you a chance to explain yourself. People like that, it's generally best for them to never even know you're in the area."

"Yeah," Joe said, still eyeing the stranger suspiciously. "But I'm not like that."

"No, I reckon you ain't," the stranger said. He chuckled again, but this time, in the middle of his laugh, he winced in pain, and he put his hand to his side.

"You all right?"

"Yeah, I'm fine. My horse threw me, that's all."

"You don't look like a man who'd be easily throw'd," Joe suggested.

"Yeah, well, sometimes things happen."

Joe continued to keep a wary eye on the man. That was when he saw blood on his side.

"You're bleeding," he said. "How'd you wind up bleeding from gettin' throw'd?"

"Well, it's this way," the man said. He pulled his jacket back as if to show his wound. Then, suddenly, a gun appeared in his hand. "I wasn't exactly throw'd," he said. "I was shot."

Joe cursed himself for his stupidity. He was suspicious of the man from the very beginning and had been keeping a close eye on him; still, the man managed, somehow, to get the drop on him.

"Who shot you?"

"I ain't exactly sure who it was," the stranger admitted. "One minute me and three of my pards was holdin' up this train, an' the next minute all hell was breakin' loose. Some passenger come offen the train with his gun blazin'. I think he kilt my three pards, an' somebody hit me an' my horse as we was ridin' away. Kilt my horse too. Left him lying about two miles back in the dark.''

"Sounds to me like you and your pards woulda been better off back in some town, drinkin' beer and sportin' the pretty girls,'' Joe said.

"Yeah, well, my pards, maybe,'' the stranger admitted. "They're lyin' back there as dead as my horse. But me, I got away.'' He patted his pockets. "And I got me over a thousand dollars of the railroad's money,'' he added. "With no one I have to share it with.''

"With a bullet in your side and a dead horse, you aren't in that good of a shape,'' Joe suggested.

"Half hour or so ago, I woulda agreed with you,'' the stranger said. "But then I seen your fire, and I figured my luck had changed. Looks like I'm goin' to be needin' your horse.''

Joe shook his head. "Sorry,'' he said. "My horse ain't for sale.''

"Don't need no bill of sale, mister. Just your horse. I plan on leavin' your carcass here. You got five seconds to make your peace.''

"Don't need to make my peace,'' Joe said. "All I need is to finish my coffee.''

"Go ahead,'' the stranger said generously. "No need of me sendin' a man to hell on an empty stomach.''

"Mind if I warm it?'' Joe asked, reaching for the pot with his left hand.

"Go ahead. Just don't get any fancy ideas about tossing the coffee in my face. If I see that pot so much as wiggle, I'm shootin'.''

"Yeah, well, you're goin' to shoot me anyway, aren't you?'' Joe replied. He began pouring coffee with his left hand and poured too much so that it splashed down over the edge of the cup, running onto his hand.

"Damn, that's hot!'' he shouted in pain, dropping the cup.

The stranger laughed. "Yeah, well, it ain't goin' to hurt too long, 'cause—''

That was as far as he got, for as Joe dropped his cup,

his hand also dipped to the pistol at his side. He pulled it and fired before the stranger caught on to what he was doing. The bullet caught the stranger in the center of his chest, knocking him down before he could react by pulling the trigger of his own pistol.

Joe cocked his pistol for a second shot, but he saw immediately that a second shot wouldn't be needed.

"Damn!" the stranger said with an expulsion of breath. "Damn, damn, you got me good with that one. Where'd you learn a trick like that?"

"I don't know," Joe said. "It just came to me, I guess." He eased the hammer down on his pistol, then knelt beside the wounded man. He could see the blood frothing at the entry hole, and he knew his bullet had penetrated the lungs. He tore off a piece of the man's shirt and stuck it in the hole to slow the bleeding, but he knew he was just wasting his time.

"No use in doin' all that," the wounded man said, indicating that he too knew it was a waste of time. "I can hear this wound suckin' air. Ain't never know'd anybody to survive a wound like that. Have you?"

"No," Joe replied.

The stranger tried to chuckle, but the attempt turned into a hacking cough. "Hell," he said. "You coulda lied to me . . . tried to make me feel better."

"Why would I want to do that? You was plannin' on killin' me, wasn't you?"

"I reckon I was, at that. Tell you what you do. You take this here money I stole . . . sure as hell ain't goin' to do me no good now . . . an' you ride on into Belle Springs an' have yourself a good time. My name's Beatie. Jared Beatie. There's a girl in Belle Springs, works at the Gilded Cage."

Beatie interrupted his talk with a coughing spasm that sprayed blood onto his beard and shirt. Finally he was able to talk again.

"She calls herself Lily Bird, but her real name is Lucy Beatie. She's my sister. I'd like you to tell her you run across me as I was dyin'. No need to tell her how I died, or that you was the one that kilt me. But I'd like her to know what happened to me.''

''I'll do that,'' Joe promised. ''Anything else I can do that'll—'' He stopped in mid-sentence when he saw that Beatie had quit breathing.

IT WAS NEARLY MIDNIGHT WHEN JOE REACHED BELLE Springs. The hoofbeats of his horse clomped hollowly as he rode into the dark town. Golden bubbles of light were splashed out onto the street, and Joe passed through them, in and out of light and shadow so that his face was now glowing, now dark.

The fact that the outlaw, Jared Beatie, wanted him to come to Belle Springs was a coincidence. In fact, Joe was going to Belle Springs anyway, in response to a telegram from his brother.

MEET ME IN BELLE SPRINGS, the telegram had read in a frugal use of words, giving no explanation as to why he wanted him there, or where they would meet.

The why of it didn't matter much to Joe. If his brother wanted to meet here in Belle Springs, that was good enough for him. And as for the where . . . well, what better place to meet than a saloon? Besides which, he might be able to locate Beatie's sister and kill two birds with one stone.

Joe guided his horse toward the brightest and loudest building in town. It seemed another fortuitous coincidence to Joe that this was the Gilded Cage.

Inside, the saloon was lighted by one huge, bright chandelier, as well as by a dozen or so kerosene lanterns. The bar was crowded, and the tables were full. At least half a dozen of the men were wearing deputy's badges, and Joe hesitated for a moment before he went any farther. Although he didn't believe there was any paper out on him or his brother at the moment, there had been plenty of paper in the past during their time with Quantrill, and immediately after the war. Therefore, being in the midst of so many lawmen was not necessarily his idea of a good time.

He noticed, however, that the others, those who were not wearing badges, seemed totally unintimidated by those who were. On the contrary, they seemed to act as if there were no such thing as disturbing the peace or public drunkenness.

"Hey!" someone shouted. "Hey, watch me do the fandango!"

The would-be dancer got up from one of the tables, then began stomping around in an imitation of a dancer. One of the other patrons pulled a pistol.

"You call that dancin'! Maybe this'll help!" He fired at the would-be dancer's feet. His second shot hit the dancer and he fell to the floor, grabbing his foot and moaning in pain.

"Hell, Jesse, I didn't mean to hit you," the shooter apologized. He got down on the floor and pulled Jesse's boot off, then wrapped the bullet hole with a handkerchief.

The shooting made very little stir in the bar. No more than two or three people even seemed to notice it.

At one table in the back, a bar girl was sitting on a cowboy's lap. At first, Joe thought she was just being a little bold with her flirting, but as he looked more closely he was shocked to see that they were actually having sex. Her skirt was spread out to provide some privacy, but it managed only to hide the actual connection. There was absolutely no doubt as to what was going on under the skirt ... that was obvious, not only by her humping motion against him, but also by the expressions on their faces. Joe had never seen anything quite so brazen, and he stared in unabashed curiosity.

"Somethin' I can do for you, cowboy?" one of the other bar girls asked, noticing him watching the man and woman back in the corner.

"What?" Joe asked.

The bar girl jutted her hip out and lifted the hem of her skirt, showing naked leg, all the way up to a red garter.

"You seem awfully interested in what Sue Ellen is doing with her gentleman friend," the bar girl said. "If you come on back into the corner with me we'll find us a chair, and I can do the same thing for you. It'll only cost you two dollars."

"Are you the one they call Lily?" Joe asked.

The girl shook her head. "No, honey, Lily don't work here no more. But whatever Lily could do for you, I can too. Why don't you come on back here with me and let me show you?"

"No, thanks," Joe said. "I've never been much for doing such a thing in a chair . . . especially in public."

The girl smiled invitingly and looked at him through cobra-hooded, smoky eyes. "Honey, doin' it in public is what makes it fun," she said. "And don't worry 'bout sittin' in a chair. I'll be the one that's doin' all the work."

"Thanks, but no thanks," Joe said again.

"Whatever you say, honey. You're the one missin' out," she said. With one last, smoldering look to make certain he hadn't changed his mind, she drifted away to accost another. A moment later, Joe saw that her solicitation had been successful, as she led a willing partner toward one of the empty chairs in the back of the crowded room.

"Are you goin' to bet, or are you just goin' to sit there with your thumb up your ass?" Joe heard someone say. When he looked around he saw a poker game in progress. The one who had issued the challenge was wearing a deputy's badge.

"I'm foldin'," the man who was challenged replied. "And I'm quittin' while I still got two coins to rub together." He raked in the small pile in front of him and stood up.

The deputy laughed. "Freeman, what you got to understand is, poker is ninety-nine percent skill and one percent luck. I always did say that's what separates the men from the boys in this game. You are a boy in a man's game."

"Yeah, well, I'll say this for you, Reeves. I never met a man who could run a bluff cooler than you," Freeman said. "But you ain't gettin' no more of my money. Not tonight, you ain't."

Freeman put his money in his pocket and walked away, leaving an empty chair. Joe looked pointedly at the chair.

"You just goin' to stand there lookin', farm boy? Or are you goin' to play?" the deputy asked.

5

"WAS HOPIN' I'D BE INVITED," JOE SAID, TAKING THE chair. Having already observed the kind of clientele frequenting the place, Joe sat in such a way as to allow him immediate access to his pistol.

"You puttin' any money on the table, or you plannin' on trying to get by on your ugly looks?" Reeves asked, and the others laughed at his joke.

"Thought I might start with this," Joe replied. He put five double eagles on the table, and the gold coins glistened brightly, contrasting sharply with the light-absorbing green cloth on top of the table.

Reeves looked at the money in surprise. "Where'd a farm boy like you get money like that?"

"Is my money good here or not?" Joe replied, without answering the question.

Reeves nodded. "Your money's good here, farm boy," he said. "Until I take it, that is," he added, laughing. Then, to the others around the table, he said, "Boys, looks like the farm boy here has decided to join us, so I propose a new deck." Reeves opened a new box of cards. He spread them out on the table, then flipped them over expertly. He was quite good with the cards, and he was making a little show of it for Joe.

"Satisfied with the deck, farm boy?" Reeves asked.

"Yeah," Joe answered. "Deal them."

Reeves shuffled the cards, and the stiff new pasteboards clicked sharply. His hands moved swiftly, folding the cards in and out until the probability of random numbers became the law of the table. He shoved the deck toward Joe. Joe cut them, then pushed them back.

"Five-card draw?"

"Suits me."

Joe lost fifteen dollars on the first hand, folding cautiously with a hand that would have been good enough to win, had he stayed in.

Reeves chuckled as he drew in the pot.

"This isn't a game for the weak of heart, farm boy," he said. "You shoulda bet that hand."

Joe lost the second hand the same way, and again Reeves laughed.

By the third hand, Joe was down thirty-five dollars, but there was over sixty dollars in the pot and he had drawn two cards to complete a heart flush. He bet five dollars.

"Careful now, mister," Reeves taunted. "You don't want to get carried away, now. I'll see your five and raise you five."

Joe made a big show of studying his hand carefully. Finally, as if only after careful consideration, he called, but didn't raise Reeves's bet.

"All right farm boy, let's see what you got," Reeves said. The deputy was holding three kings, and he laughed when he saw Joe's hand.

"A flush? You mean to tell me you had a flush and all you did was call?"

"I was afraid you might've had a flush with a bigger card," Joe said. "I like to be certain about things. As you can see, it pays off." Joe raked in the pot. He was now forty dollars ahead of when he sat down.

"It pays off, does it? You're a lousy forty dollars ahead, and you think it's paying off?"

Reeves's vanity was piqued at the thought of a farm boy taking the pot. What he didn't realize was that he was reacting exactly as Joe wanted him to react.

"I'm going to ante the limit this time," Joe said, sliding some money forward. "Ten dollars."

"Well, you're getting into some heavy money now," Reeves teased. "What do you say we up the ante a little?"

"Up the ante?" Joe replied.

"Sure. You say your system is paying off. Why don't we just up the ante and test it?"

"All right," Joe said hesitantly, as if he were being taken in by Reeves.

"That's more like it," Reeves said. He shoved the cards across the table to Joe. "Here. It's your deal."

When Joe picked up the cards, he felt them as he began shuffling, checking for pinpricks and uneven corners. They seemed to be playing with an honest deck. He smiled. Evidently Reeves was so sure of himself that he felt no need to cheat in this game.

Joe dealt the cards. The betting was quite spirited, and within a few moments the pot was over two hundred dollars.

"Now, farm boy, it's time for the nut-cutting," Reeves snarled. "I'm afraid it's going to cost you to see what I have." He slid a stack of chips to the center of the table. "Fifty dollars."

Reeves's bet was high enough to run everyone else out of the game, and he chuckled as it had the desired effect. He looked across the table at Joe, who had not yet folded.

"You stayin'?" the deputy asked.

Joe stroked his chin. "I thought I might," he said. There was a subtle change in Joe's demeanor, one that sent a tiny twinge of doubt through Reeves.

"Well, come on, we ain't got all night," Reeves said. "What are you going to do?"

"I think I'll just see your fifty and raise it one hundred and fifty," Joe said. He had to take more gold double eagles from his pocket to make the bet, and he dropped the gold coins on the pile in the center.

Reeves's mouth opened and he looked at Joe in surprise. "What kind of hand do you have, mister?" he asked.

"A pretty good one, I think," Joe answered. He put the cards down in front of him, four to one side, and one off by itself.

"Son of a bitch! He's got four of a kind," someone said. "Look at the way he put his cards down. He's got four of a kind!"

"I'll tell you this. There's over four hundred dollars in that pot," another said.

By now the stakes of the game were high enough to attract the attention of everyone else in the saloon, and there were several men standing around the table, watching the game with intense interest. Even the bar girls—those who weren't working on the back chairs—had come over to see what was going on.

Whispered questions were passed back and forth. Would the deputy call or raise? Did the farm boy actually have four of a kind?

"Call his hand, Reeves," someone said. "I can tell by lookin' at him that he's bluffin'. Call his hand."

"It's my money you're talkin' about," Reeves replied. "It'll cost me a hunnert 'n fifty dollars to call."

"You got it, ain't you?"

"Not to throw away," Reeves said nervously. "Don't forget, this is the fella who wouldn't even raise a flush."

Joe's face was totally impassive.

"What are you goin' to do, Deputy?" one of the by-standers asked. "Like you told the farm boy here, you can't take all night."

"All right, goddamn it, the pot's yours," Reeves growled, throwing his cards on the table. He had a full house, aces over jacks. "What have you got?"

Joe's cards stayed facedown on the table just the way he'd left them, four in one pile, one in the other. He reached out to rake in the pot.

"I said what have you got?" Reeves asked again. He reached for Joe's cards, but Joe caught his wrist with a vise grip.

"You didn't pay to see them," Joe said.

With his other hand, Reeves slid a stack of chips across the table. Joe saw that there were at least fifty dollars in the stack. "Is that enough to buy a look at your cards?" he asked.

"All right," Joe replied. "If you want to." He let go of Reeves's wrist, and Reeves turned up the cards. Instead of four of a kind, there were two small pairs.

"What?" Reeves gasped. "You beat me with two pairs?"

Most of the onlookers had a good laugh, but the deputy stared them down until they were silent.

"You jerked a cinch into me, farm boy," Reeves said. "I don't like that."

"You said it yourself, mister," Joe replied. "Poker is ninety-nine percent skill and one percent luck. I reckon you were a little short on both."

With a frustrated shout of anger, Reeves drove a right into Joe's jaw, taking him by surprise and knocking him back against the table behind him. Reeves wasn't quite as large a man as Joe, but he had a leathery toughness about him, and he was a skilled barroom fighter. He also had a killer instinct, and such an instinct served him exceptionally well in a fight where there were no rules.

Reeves was confident, but he was no fool. He knew he would have to get in a telling blow quickly, so while Joe was still a little groggy, he sent a whistling punch into Joe's Adam's apple, and followed that immediately with a punch to the groin. Joe dropped to his knees, and Reeves drew back his fist for one final, telling blow, to put him away.

Joe saw Reeves get set for a roundhouse right. At the last possible instant, Joe jerked his head to one side. Reeves's hand slid past, finding only empty air. At the same time, Joe sent a short, brutal right against Reeves's belly, drawing a loud grunt and sending the deputy backward with quick little steps to keep from going down. Joe took that opportunity to jump to his feet.

Reeves realized now that he had lost his advantage. His only hope had been to take Joe out with surprise, but Joe had taken the best Reeves had to offer and was now coming at him on even terms. Desperately, Reeves sent a left jab toward Joe, but Joe slipped it easily and countered with a short right hook to Reeves's jaw. It was only the second time Joe had swung at Reeves, but both punches had landed with telling effectiveness.

Reeves tried another left jab, hoping to set Joe up for a roundhouse right. Joe took the jab in order to get in close. He hooked Reeves with a left, then caught him flush with a hard right, and Reeves went down.

Reeves struggled to his feet, but now he had completely given up any idea of winning a fistfight. Instead, he went for his gun.

Joe smiled. He had been expecting this, and he was ready for it. He didn't even bother to reach for his own gun. Instead, he had a clear, unobstructed shot at Reeves's jaw, and he put everything into a roundhouse right which lifted Reeves from the floor, then sent him crashing through a table. He lay on the floor with his mouth open, his jaws slack, and his eyes closed, totally unconscious.

Suddenly the lights went out for Joe, and he fell to the floor, facedown, as unconscious as the man he had just bested. Standing behind Joe were two other deputies. One of them was holding the remnants of the chair he had just broken over Joe's head.

"Big son of a bitch, isn't he?" the deputy with the broken chair said.

"Yeah," the other answered. "It's going to be a load, carrying him down to the jail."

THE NEXT MORNING, WIN COULTER, SMOKING A CHEROOT and wearing only his hat, stood at the window of the room he had taken upstairs at the Desert Flower, looking down on Belle Springs' Main Street. It was a little after seven, and at this hour of the day, the town had some of the look of industriousness about it that Doc had spoken of the night before.

Two freight wagons, heavily laden with copper ore, rumbled slowly down the street, headed for the smelter. Across the street the storekeeper was sweeping his front porch. A little farther down the street, at the apothecary, the druggist turned the CLOSED sign around to read OPEN in the front window of his establishment.

"What do you see?" Claire asked from the bed behind him.

"Couple of wagons, a couple of storekeepers," Win answered without turning around.

"No," Claire said. "I mean, what do you really see? Do you see trouble coming?"

Win turned away from the window. Claire was in the feather bed, covered by a brightly colored, patchwork quilt. The quilt held a distinctive aroma; soap, lilac, and a hint of her musk. She had invited him up last night, and they had explored each other's bodies until the small hours of morning.

"I never look for trouble," Win said.

Claire smiled. "You strike me as the kind of man who doesn't have to look for it," she said. "I have a feeling it just naturally comes your way."

Claire sat up and stretched. When she did, the quilt fell down from her shoulders, exposing her small but well-formed breasts. Smiling, Win returned to the bed, then sat down beside her. She shivered as his fingers traced the rims of the globes.

"My," she said. "You do know how to wake a girl up. But you're still dressed," she added, looking at his hat.

"The important part of me isn't dressed," Win replied, taking her hand and putting it on his stiffening rod.

"You're right," she said, closing her fingers around the hot shaft. "The important part of you isn't dressed."

Win leaned forward to touch one of her taut nipples with a kiss, then his tongue circled it again and again as his hands kneaded the pliant breasts.

"I knew when I saw you," Claire said. "When you first came into the saloon, I knew."

"You knew what?" Win asked, his voice somewhat muffled by his task.

"I knew that you would be good," she said. "The best,"

she added. She began to writhe and moan as his mouth moved from nipple to nipple, teasing them until they were stone hard.

Win pulled the quilt off her, then continued to work on her with his lips and tongue, sucking the nipples, then letting his tongue trail down her belly until it reached the carrot-red forest at the junction of her legs. He probed there, until his tongue found her nether lips.

"That's good," she said, moaning. "That's real good, but I want more. I want this." She was still holding him, and she squeezed gently, then began moving it, showing him what she wanted. She spread her legs in an invitation for him to crawl between them.

Win raised himself up, then looked down at her. Her hair was fanned on the pillow, her green eyes were half shut and smoldering.

"Give it to me, please," she said. "You know what I want."

Win moved into position, then let her make the connection between them. He felt the head slip into her moist box, and he wanted to plunge himself all the way in, but Claire was a skilled practitioner of erotic arts and she knew how to produce an even greater ardor. She did this by tightening and loosening, then tightening and loosening her pelvic muscles, allowing him to come in slowly, inch by swollen inch.

Then, just as Win was nearly driven mad with her erotic teasing, her own desires took over, and she put her hands on his butt and drew him toward her, so tightly that he could feel his balls sinking into her pubic hair.

"All of it!" she moaned through clenched teeth. "I want all of it!"

Claire reached a shuddering climax, kissing Win passionately to bring him to an equal point. Her hands slid along his naked shoulders and back until his lean form quivered, every muscle in his body was as tight as steel, and his breath was heavy with pure satisfaction.

It was at that precise moment that a heavy banging on the door invaded their private world.

"Claire! Claire!" a man's voice called. Win recognized it as the bartender's voice. "Claire, you in there?"

Win rolled off Claire. Unseen by Claire, he reached over to the gun belt, which had lain on the chair within quick grasp all night long, and eased his pistol out of his holster.

"I'm in here, Harry," Claire said, her voice somewhat breathy from the recent exertion.

"Is Coulter with you? Or did he leave during the night?"

Claire looked over at Win before she answered. He had stepped into his pants and was now pulling on his boots. He mouthed the word, "Why?"

"Why do you want to know?" she asked.

" 'Cause there's a fella come into town durin' the middle of the night that I think Coulter's goin' to want to know about."

Win finished putting on his boots, then stepped over to the door and jerked it open. He was holding his pistol in his hand and that, plus the sudden opening of the door, startled Harry, and he jumped back in alarm.

Win looked out into the hall to make certain Harry was alone, then he stepped back from the door.

"Come on in," he said.

Harry stepped into the room. Seeing that Claire was still naked, though beginning to get dressed, he cleared his throat, then turned aside.

"For heaven's sake, Harry, you've seen me naked before," Claire said with a chuckle.

"Not with another man around," Harry said.

"Who's this I'm goin' to want to know about?" Win asked.

"You got a brother named Joe?"

"I do."

"Then you better get down to the jail fast. Word I got is, Pendrake's aimin' to hang him."

6

"HELLO, LITTLE BROTHER," WIN SAID.

Joe, who had been asleep on his bunk in the cell, opened his eyes. Seeing Win standing on the other side of the bars, he grinned.

"Win," he said. "It's good to see you."

"It's like Ma and Pa told me when we were kids," Win said. " 'Son, don't take your eyes off your little brother for even a minute,' they said. 'Because, sure as you do, he's goin' to get in trouble.' They sure knew what they were talking about."

"I reckon they did," Joe answered.

A man, wearing a deputy's badge, overhearing the conversation, came back to the jail cell to see what was going on. The deputy had a black eye and a badly swollen lip.

"You do this, Little Brother?" Win asked, nodding toward the deputy.

"I reckon so," Joe replied easily. "His name is Reeves. He ain't much of a card player, he's a terrible fighter, and he's an even worse sport. Deputy Reeves, this is my brother, Win Coulter."

"Well, Mr. Win Coulter," Reeves snarled, "you got here just in time to see your brother hang."

"When was the trial held?" Win asked.

"The sheriff held it last night, right after we brought him in."

"That a fact, Joe?" Win asked.

Joe chuckled, then shook his head. "Well, you couldn't prove it one way or the other by me, Win. I was out when they brought me in. When I woke up this mornin', they told me I was goin' to hang."

"The hell you say," Win replied. "What'd you find him guilty of?" he asked the deputy.

"I'll answer that question for you, Mr. Coulter," Pendrake said, coming into the cell area from his office. "Your brother is guilty of train robbery."

"Train robbery?" Win replied. "What train did he rob?"

"You ought to know, Coulter. You were on it. Your brother's the one that got away."

"Is that a fact? Tell me, Pendrake, what made you come up with that idea?"

"When we brought him in last night, he had seven hundred nineteen dollars on him."

"It should be over a thousand," Joe said. "Reeves here took back the money I won from him in the poker game last night."

"The way I figure it, the only way he coulda got his hands on that kind of cash was if he was the fourth train robber . . . the one that got away with all the money."

"I told him I got the money from selling a string of horses," Joe explained. "He doesn't seem to believe me."

"Pendrake, I saw the fourth man riding off into the dark. It wasn't my brother."

"I'd expect you to say something like that," Pendrake replied. "Not only to save your brother, but also because I'm still not convinced you wasn't a part of it."

"There's an easy way to get to the bottom of this," Win suggested. "All you have to do is talk to the express man on the train. He got a good look at the fourth man. He could tell you it wasn't Joe.''

''Maybe he could and maybe he couldn't,'' Pendrake replied. ''But the thing is, he ain't here, and I don't have time to wait around for him.''

''The way I figure it, this doesn't have anything to do with the train robbery, Win,'' Joe said. ''I figure they have me in here 'cause I beat the deputy at poker.''

''It *is* why they have you here,'' Win replied. He looked at Pendrake. ''Pendrake, they say the robber got away with twelve hundred dollars, right?''

''That's right.''

''But you also say my brother only had seven hundred dollars on him.''

''That's right too. Figured he's already spent some of it.''

''In one night?''

''Don't take a free spender too long to spend five hundred dollars.''

''Yeah, well, there's one thing you're overlooking. If Joe and I were partners in a robbery that netted twelve hundred dollars and he showed up here with only seven hundred, you wouldn't have to hang him. I would shoot the son of a bitch myself.''

Unexpectedly, Pendrake laughed. ''You know,'' he said. ''You just might be the kind who would do that.''

''Damned right I would,'' Win replied. ''And if you hang him, I'm going to shoot you.''

''You'd better watch who you're threatening,'' Pendrake stuttered, the smile leaving his face.

''I'm not threatening, I'm promising,'' Win said. ''Now let him go. You know damned well he didn't have anything to do with that train robbery.''

Pendrake glared at Win for a moment, then once again he smiled, though this time the smile was more forced than before.

''All right, maybe he didn't have anything to do with robbin' the train,'' Pendrake agreed. ''But he did half kill one of my deputies last night in a fight over a card game.''

"Yeah!" Reeves said. "It doesn't matter whether the son of a bitch robbed the train or not. He's goin' to hang for attempted—" That was as far as Reeves got before Win drew his pistol then brought it down sharply on the deputy's head. Reeves let out a yelp of pain, then took a couple of steps back as blood began to run down his forehead, between his eyes.

"What the hell?" Reeves barked. "Pendrake, did you see that?"

"You his wet nurse, Pendrake?" Win asked derisively. "If he can't handle himself any better than this, looks to me like the thing to do is get rid of him."

Pendrake looked over at Reeves, who was now blotting the blood with his handkerchief. The fresh blood added to the black eye and swollen lip from last night made him a pitiful sight indeed.

Pendrake nodded. "You're right," he said. "Reeves, leave your badge on my desk and get out of here."

"What?" Reeves questioned in disbelief.

"You heard me. You're fired."

"Now, wait a minute, Pendrake," Reeves protested. "You can't do that."

"Yeah, I can, and I just did," Pendrake said.

Reeves glared at Win for a long moment before sullenly taking off his badge, then walking over and laying it on Pendrake's desk. He pointed at Win. "You ain't heard the last of me, mister," he said.

Win took a step toward him and Reeves jumped, then, without another word, turned and left, slamming the door behind him.

Win watched the door slam, then turned toward Pendrake. "May I have my brother now?" he asked, nodding toward the cell.

"You can have him. I guess it was all just a little misunderstanding. No hard feelin's, I hope." Pendrake walked over to the wall and took a ring of keys from a hook, then came back and opened the cell door. "You're free to go, Coulter."

"What about my money?" Joe asked, picking his hat up from the bed.

"Oh, yes, the seven hundred dollars."

"Seven hundred and nineteen," Joe said. "Plus the money I won in the poker game."

Pendrake took a roll of money from his pocket and peeled off seven one-hundred-dollar bills, and handed them to Joe.

"Don't know anything about the poker game money," Pendrake said. "And you can count the nineteen dollars as your fine. That is, unless . . . ?" He let the sentence hang.

"Unless what?"

"Unless the two of you'd like to wear deputies' badges. If you want it, the job's yours," Pendrake said.

"No, thank you," Win said. "I don't think either one of us has ever seen ourselves as lawmen."

Pendrake laughed. "Yeah, I know what you mean. I never figured on being one either. But this is too sweet an opportunity to pass up."

"Come on, Joe," Win said, starting for the door.

"I suppose you two will be leavin' town now," Pendrake said.

Win and Joe stopped, and Win looked back toward the sheriff.

"Not for a while," Win answered. "We've got a business to run."

"A business?" Joe asked, surprised at his brother's announcement. "What sort of business?"

"The saloon business, Little Brother," Win said. "You and I are the new owners of the Desert Flower."

"We own a saloon?" Joe said, smiling broadly. "Well, now, what do you think of that?"

"Are you telling me Quartermouse sold it to you?" Pendrake asked. "It's strange that he would do that, especially after he turned me down cold. How is it that he sold it to you?"

"I didn't exactly buy it. I won it in a poker game."

Suddenly, Pendrake laughed out loud. "So that's how he got rid of it," he said. "Well, I hate to be the one to tell you this, Mr. Coulter, but the truth is, you just got took. That saloon is losing money, and has been losing money for a long time. I guess, maybe, you don't know who your competition is."

"Why, it's you, isn't it?" Win asked. "You do own the Gilded Cage, don't you?"

Pendrake blinked, surprised that Win not only knew but apparently didn't seem to care.

"Yes," he said. "Yes, I do own it. And you may have noticed that the Gilded Cage does a lot of business, whereas the Desert Flower doesn't serve enough customers to pay for the kerosene it takes to keep the lamps burning."

"I have a feeling all that is going to change," Win said.

"How do you plan to do that?"

Win smiled easily. "Like you said, Pendrake, you're my competition. You don't really expect me to give away all my secrets, do you?"

Pendrake's eyes narrowed, and he pointed at Win. "Coulter, I think maybe I should tell you that I've got things goin' my way in this town. I sort of like it like that. I wouldn't look too kindly on someone who came along and tried to change things."

"No, I don't suppose you would," Win replied.

"IT'S GOOD TO SEE YOU AGAIN, LITTLE BROTHER," WIN said as the two men walked across the street from the sheriff's office, toward the Desert Flower saloon. The appellation "Little Brother" seemed incongruous when one saw the two men together, because Joe, though two years younger, was six inches taller and fifty pounds heavier than his older brother.

"Well, I have to admit I was sort of glad to see your ugly face too," Joe said. "Especially when the sheriff started talking about hanging me for robbin' that train."

Win laughed. "It would've been funny, wouldn't it," he said, "to get hung for a train you didn't rob, when there are so many that we have?"

"Oh, yeah," Joe said, putting his hand to his neck. "I woulda laughed all the way to hell. But the last laugh woulda been on you, Big Brother. 'Cause I've got that train money hidden in my saddle, and you would've never known it.''

Win stopped in the middle of the street and looked over at Joe.

''What did you say?''

''That train that was robbed? I've got the money,'' Joe said easily.

''How the hell did that happen? I know you weren't there. I was on that train. There were only four robbers. I killed three, and I saw the fourth as he was getting away. It definitely wasn't you.''

''Well, somebody shot him as he was getting away,'' Joe said. ''They hit him . . . and his horse.''

''It must have been that Loomis fella,'' Win said. ''His own partner shot him for riding off. How did you wind up with the money?''

Joe described his encounter with the robber Jared Beatie, telling how Beatie gave him the money as he was dying. ''I hope you aren't goin' to say we have to give it back,'' he concluded.

Win laughed. ''Now, tell me, Joe,'' he said. ''Have I ever done a dumb thing like that?''

CLAIRE, HARRY, AND DOC MET WIN AND JOE AT THE front door of the Desert Flower.

''Folks, I'd like you to meet my little brother Joe,'' Win said, introducing him to the others.

''Saints be praised, he ain't hung!'' Harry said. ''Now, just how the hell did you do that?''

''I appealed to Pendrake's regard for human life,'' Win said.

''Regard for human life? Ha! When did that son of a bitch ever have any regard for human life?'' Doc asked.

''I guess it depends on the human involved,'' Joe replied. ''Win told him if I hung, he would shoot him.''

Harry laughed out loud. ''Good for you, Mr. Coulter,'' he said. Then to Joe, ''I'm glad you didn't get hung, Joe, but it would almost be worth it to see Pendrake shot down in the street like the dog he is.''

"Well, I'm sorry to disappoint you," Joe said, and the others laughed.

"This calls for a drink, on the house," Harry said. "Step up to the bar.''

"Tell me, Harry, shouldn't you clear it with the owner before you start giving away free drinks?" Win teased.

"Well, if Mr. Quartermouse was here, I'd ask him," Harry said. "But he's nowhere around. Besides, he owes me so much in back wages that if he said anything, I'd just tell him to take it out of my pay.''

"That's very generous of you, Harry," Win said. "But the truth is, Quartermouse isn't the owner anymore.''

"What do you mean?" Harry asked. Suddenly his face went pale. "Good Lord, you aren't going to tell me that Mr. Quartermouse sold out to Pendrake, are you?''

"What if he has?''

"If he has, then more than one drink is free," Harry replied. "I'll give away everything in the saloon until there's not a drop of liquor left. Then I'm getting out of town.''

Win chuckled. "Relax," he said. "Pendrake doesn't own this saloon.''

"Then who does?''

"I do," Win said. "That is, my brother and I do." He took the deed from his pocket and showed it to Harry and the others.

Harry took the document from Win and examined it for a moment, then he showed it to Doc.

"Doc, what do you think of this? Is it on the up-and-up?''

Doc looked at the deed and at Quartermouse's signature. "It looks like the real thing to me, Harry," he said.

"It is the real thing," Win said. "I won it in a poker game several days ago.''

"You mean, when you came in here last night, you already owned this place?" Claire asked.

"Yes.''

"And you didn't say a word?"

"I wasn't sure how everyone would take it," Win replied. "I didn't know how you would feel about me taking the saloon from Quartermouse."

"Mr. Quartermouse is a good man," Harry said. "And I didn't mind working for him. But he wasn't the kind of man who could stand up to Harley Pendrake. If you hadn't won the saloon from him in a poker game, it would have wound up belonging to the sheriff. So, all things considered, I think it's best this way."

"I'm sure Mr. Coulter appreciates your vote of confidence," Doc said. "But how can you be so sure it's for the best? You don't know him."

"Maybe not," Harry said. "But I sure as hell know Harley Pendrake."

"I say it's for the best," Claire cooed. "I haven't known Mr. Coulter long, but I have, as they say, known him well. He has my vote."

Doc stuck out his hand. "Well, Mr. Coulter, if you can win over these two, then you've got me as well," he said. "Welcome to Belle Springs."

"Now, what about that drink you said was on the house?" Joe asked.

"Right away," Harry said, pouring whiskey into a glass. "But, technically speaking, it isn't on the house anymore. It already belongs to you."

"You mean it's already my drink?" Joe asked.

"That's what I mean," Harry said. He slid the shot glass across the bar to Joe.

Joe tossed the drink down, then wiped his mouth with the back of his hand.

"Damn, it's just as I thought," Joe said.

"What's that?"

"Somehow a drink on the house doesn't taste as good if it already belongs to me."

7

"Harry, if you had to guess, what would you say would be the best way to bring business back to the Desert Flower?" Win asked.

"That's easy," Harry answered. "Find some way to not charge folks the sheriff's tax."

"Good idea," Win said. "All right, from now on, no more tax."

"If we do that, how are we going to handle Pendrake?"

"Don't you worry about that," Win said. "I'll handle Pendrake."

"I have another suggestion," Claire said.

"All right, let's hear it."

"Maybe we could get some of the girls back. A lot of customers like girls to drink with and, uh . . . visit," she said, searching for an acceptable euphemism. "Before Pendrake we had the best ones, all friendly and pretty. Then, when the business died, they had to leave. A lot of them went to work at the Gilded Cage, but when they saw what Pendrake wanted them to do, most of them quit."

"Why? What did he want them to do there that is different from what they did here?"

"You mean you haven't been in the Gilded Cage?"

"Nope. I came here first thing, soon as I got to town."

"Well, uh, I'm sort of embarrassed to tell you what he wants his girls to do."

"Are you talking about the chairs in the back of the room?" Joe asked.

"Yes."

Win looked confused. "I still don't know what you mean. What are you talking about, the chairs?"

"The whores over there take care of, uh, their *business* in chairs," Joe said.

"In chairs?" Win was still confused.

"Yes," Joe said. "In the back of the room . . . in plain view of everyone, they, uh . . . fornicate," he added.

"My God. Why would they do that?"

"Pendrake believes that if the men see the girls going about their business out in the open like that, they'll get all excited and the girls will do even more business. And, since he gets three fourths of everything they get, it makes a lot of money for him."

"Three fourths? Is that normal?"

"I think a normal fee is about forty percent," Doc said.

Win looked at Joe. "Joe, you didn't . . ."

"No!" Joe said quickly, answering before his brother finished the question. "Come on, Win, you know me better than that."

"I thought I did," he said. "I just wanted to make sure, that's all. I'm sorry, Claire, I interrupted. You were saying something about the girls who left here."

"Yes. I was thinking that if we could get those girls back . . ."

"An excellent idea," Win said. "Do you think you could get in touch with them?"

"Yes, I'm sure I could."

"Then do it."

"Hot damn!" Joe said excitedly. "Win, do you realize what this means? We not only own a saloon, hell, we own a whorehouse too!"

"Not exactly," Win said, when he saw Claire wince.

"Oh, sorry, Claire," Joe said. "Didn't mean nothin' bad by it."

"I know," Claire said. She smiled. "And, much as I try and doctor it up with words like 'soiled dove,' 'buffalo girl,' and 'lady of the line,' I am, after all, a whore."

"Yeah, but you are a good whore," Joe said, trying to make up for his blunder. "Uh, what I mean is . . ."

Win laughed. "Leave it be, Little Brother. You're just making it worse. She knows what you mean."

Claire put her hand on Joe's arm. "Don't worry," she said. "I'm not offended."

"Good. 'Cause I sure didn't want to offend you," Joe said. "Oh, uh, these girls who used to work here. Would one of them be calling herself Lily Bird, by any chance?"

"Yes," Claire answered. "Why, do you know Lily?"

Joe shook his head. "I don't know her," he said. "But I knew someone who did know her, and he asked me to look her up."

"Lily is a very sweet person," Claire said. "And a dear friend of mine. She would be a wonderful person to work here," she added. "She's very pretty and she gets along very well with everyone."

"See if you can get her, will you?" Joe said.

"I'll be glad to."

Win looked at himself in the mirror behind the bar. "If we're planning to have a lot of women in here, then I need to look a little better," he said. "Is there a barbershop near?"

"Leave it to my brother to be the handsome one," Joe said. He lifted his arm and sniffed his armpit, then made a face. "Not sure how handsome I can look, but I could sure smell a mite better if I had a bath."

"We've got a tub here," Claire said. "Your brother used it last night," she added as she and Win exchanged a private smile.

"Yeah, I'll just bet he did," Joe said. "Well, lead me to it. I'll see what I can do about getting a little more presentable."

"The barbershop?" Win asked.

"Oh. There's one down at the far end of the street, on this side, just before you get to the railroad tracks," Doc said. "The barber's name is Clem Beale."

"Is he any good?"

"He's the finest barber in town," Doc replied enthusiastically.

Harry laughed.

"You don't agree?" Win asked, questioning Harry's laugh.

"Oh, I agree, all right," Harry said. "Seein' as how Clem is the *only* barber in town." He laughed again.

SHORTLY AFTER WIN LEFT TO GET HIS SHAVE AND HAIR-cut, Joe found himself in the back of the Desert Flower saloon, sitting in a large brass bathtub, happily scrubbing away the residue of his days on the trail. His dirty clothes had been given over to Ling Lee, owner of the laundry, and a clean pair of trousers and a shirt hung across the back of a nearby chair. A cigar was elevated at a jaunty angle, and he was trying to wash his back while at the same time singing, "The dew is on the grass, Lorena . . ."

"If you'll stop that infernal racket, Joe, I'll introduce you to Miss Lily Bird," a woman's voice said. "You did say you wanted to meet her."

Surprised that a woman had come into his bathroom, Joe looked around to see Claire and another woman standing just inside. The other woman was a full-bodied blonde, nearly a head taller than Claire. She had high cheekbones and sparkling blue eyes, and, like Claire, she was smiling in amusement at the scene before her.

"Well, now, ladies," Joe said, unperturbed by their intrusion upon his bath. "Are you telling me you don't have an appreciation for fine music?"

"Is that what you call it? I've heard coyotes sing better," Lily said. To his surprise, she came over to kneel beside the bathtub, then took the cloth from him and started washing his back.

"Ahh," Joe said in blissful appreciation. "A little more

to the left, if you don't mind. There, that's it! And, yes, I do call it singing. My horse liked it.''

"Only reason it never complained is because the poor dumb animal can't talk," Lily said as she continued to scrub his back.

"Look, woman, if it's a job you're wantin', you've a poor way of impressing your employer."

"Is that a fact?" Lily said. She dropped the cloth in the water and stood up. "Well, if rudeness is the way you treat your employees, I'm not all that sure I want to work for you."

"Now, hold it, hold it, let's not get too hasty, here," Joe said. He smiled. "I've never really been a businessman before. Could be, I don't really know how to act."

"It could be," Lily agreed.

"I'm sorry. I'd love to have you working here."

"That's more like it," Lily said. She knelt again, and again picked up the washcloth and began scrubbing his back.

"Ah, that feels good, damned good," Joe said. "You know, Lily, you wouldn't even have to be a whore. You could make a good living just scrubbing backs."

Lily laughed heartily and squeezed the washcloth out over Joe's head, letting some of the soapy water run down over his face.

"Watch what you're doing, woman! You'll put out my cigar!" Joe complained.

"And why not?" Lily asked in a teasing voice. "It would clear the air of all this foul smoke."

Joe grinned and dunked his cigar in the water to extinguish it, then tossed it aside. "Listen, have you had your lunch yet?"

"No, I haven't."

"Harry's having his cook fry a chicken for me. Would you like to join me?"

"Harry's going to kill one of his chickens? I'm amazed," Lily said. "The way he fusses over them, you'd think they were his pets or something."

Joe smiled. "Well, now that I'm a substantial citizen of

the community, I suppose Harry is trying to impress me.''

"And are you trying to impress me?" Lily asked.

"Could be," Joe said. He laughed. "But, Lord, I hope Harry's not trying to impress me for the same reason I'm trying to impress you.''

Both Lily and Claire, who had not yet left, laughed.

The door opened again, and this time Doc came in. He was carrying a tray upon which sat a bottle and a glass. "Harry said you ordered this," Doc said.

"Yeah, I did. Thanks, Doc.''

Behind Doc, a huge, bald-headed man with a scar twisting its way across his flat face came in.

"Your lunch is ready," the cook said. His voice sounded like a train engine letting off steam.

Joe, still sitting in the bathtub, looked up at the growing crowd of people standing around him. "Uh . . . thanks," he said.

"Mistee Coulter, your clothes be ready one hour," Ling Lee said, coming into the room then. Ling Lee was the Chinese laundryman who had picked up Joe's dirty clothes a short time earlier.

"Now, wait just a damn minute here!" Joe said. "What the hell! Is there a sign outside the door saying this is the stage depot? I'm trying to take a bath here."

"Hell, we can all see that, Joe," Harry called mirthfully from the saloon, and his yell was followed by a raucous chorus of laughter. Joe craned his neck to see beyond the people gathered around the tub, and realized that because the door was standing wide open, he was, indeed, visible to any of the saloon patrons who cared to look in his direction.

"Doc?"

"Yes, Joe?" Doc replied, barely able to restrain his laughter.

"Leave my drink and get back to tending sick folks, will you?"

"I will, but this is more fun," Doc said.

"And you, cook, what's your name?"

"The name's Payson," the cook said with another expulsion of steam.

"All right, Payson, you put my food on a table out there, and set it for two. Miss Bird will be joining me for lunch."

Payson nodded, then started to carry the basket of chicken out with him.

"Wait a minute," Joe called, and when Payson stopped, Joe reached into the basket to pull out a drumstick.

"Now, you, Chinaman, you ain't washin' my clothes if you're in here. Get back to work."

The Chinaman bowed slightly, then withdrew. Now only Claire and Lily remained.

"Claire, you go too," Joe said. He smiled. "Lily, you can finish washing my back."

Lily smiled back at him and shook her head. "I think I had better see to it that the table is set for our lunch," she said. "I'm sure you can handle your own bath from here on out."

Barely suppressing their giggles, the two women followed the men out of the bathroom and closed the door behind them. Joe found himself alone once more. He stared at the door for a moment longer, then shrugged, took a bite of his drumstick, and raised one foot to wash, continuing his bath.

As WIN WALKED DOWN THE STREET HEADED FOR THE BARbershop, he passed the *Belle Springs Courier*. A sign on the window read: "Belle Springs's only newspaper, always independent, never neutral." When Win looked through the door he saw a man on his knees, with a screwdriver, working on the press.

"Problem?" Win asked.

The man looked up. "Oh, good," he said. "I was hoping someone would come along. Hold the tympanum for me while I tighten it, will you?"

"Hold the what?"

"This hinged cover here," the man explained.

Win held the cover while the man began making an adjustment. "I'm Ed Randol, the editor," the man said as he worked. "The Washington Hand Press is perhaps the sturdiest press ever built," he continued. "But even it requires a modicum of maintenance if it is to be kept in proper function. There, that should do it."

Randol stood up, moved the tympanum over the bed, and raised it up half a dozen times to test it. Then he wiped his hands on his apron.

"You're Win Coulter, aren't you?" Randol asked. "The one who came in on the train last night?"

"Yes."

"Pendrake offered you a job as one of his deputies, but you turned him down. I'd like to shake your hand for that."

"How did you know that?" Win asked. "It just happened."

"I'm a newspaperman, Mr. Coulter. I have a way of finding out these things," Randol said. He smiled. "For example, I know that you and your brother are the new owners of the Desert Flower saloon, and that you are not going to charge your customers a tax."

Win chuckled. "You *do* have a way of finding out things." He nodded toward the paper. "Will you be printing that in the paper?"

"It's news," Randol said. He smiled. "It's also advertising for you, but don't worry, I won't be charging you anything."

"Thanks," Win said.

"On behalf of the citizens of the community," Randol said, "the *good* citizens," he added, "I want to welcome you to Belle Springs. I have a feeling that if you stand up to Pendrake, a few of the others will as well."

"If you and the others feel that way, why haven't you stood up to him before now?" Win asked. "Why have you let him run roughshod over you for so long?"

"You ever seen a herd of cattle being moved, Mr. Coulter?"

"Yes, of course."

"Have you ever noticed how it is easier, sometimes, to get an entire herd to do what you want, than it is to get one cow? See, when a cow is all by itself, it thinks for itself. But when it's in a herd, it waits for someone else to do the thinking.

"I've got a theory that people are pretty much the same way," Randol continued. "Take this town, for example. There are several people in this town who fought bravely during the war. Individually, very few of them are cowards. But put them all together in a town, and they become just like a herd of cattle. No one wants to be the one to make the first move."

"You might be right," Win said.

"Might be? Hell, I know I'm right. That's what happened at Lawrence."

"What?" Win said sharply.

"Lawrence, Kansas. It's a place Quantrill raided, during the war."

"What do you know about it?" Win asked.

"I was publisher of the *Lawrence Gazette*," Randol said. "I was there."

"I thought all the men of Lawrence were killed. How is it that you were spared?"

"I hid, Mr. Coulter," Randol said. "When Quantrill and his gang came riding in, shooting down every man and boy in sight, I made an individual decision. I went down into the cellar and hid. You didn't get all of us."

"What?"

"I said, you didn't get all of us. I am right, aren't I? You were there, weren't you?"

"Did you see me there?"

"No," Randol admitted. "But I believe you were there. Let me show you something." Randol walked over to the side of the room, to the type-table, then began rummaging through several of the drawers, pulling things out, obviously looking for something. "Ah, here it is," he said with a note of triumph. He pulled a yellowed piece of paper from the drawer, unfolded it, then showed it to Win. The darkly printed words showed clearly through the yellow and the deep creases.

Wanted
DEAD OR ALIVE
The Brothers
WIN AND JOE COULTER
Known riders with the late Confederate
Guerrilla
QUANTRILL
$5,000 REWARD

"You *are* the same Win Coulter, are you not?" Randol asked. "And your brother is the same Joe Coulter?"

Win nodded. "We're the same," he said. He pointed at the circular. "That paper has been withdrawn, though. There is no longer a reward out for me."

Randol chuckled. "Not in Texas," he said. "But I expect you'd still find an unpleasant welcome if you took a ride up into Kansas."

"I expect so. I don't understand, Randol. If you know this about me, and if you were on the other side . . . especially in Kansas, what makes you so willing to accept my brother and me now?"

"That was then and this is now," Randol said. "War brings out the best in people . . . and the worst. I expect Lawrence is something we'd all like to put behind us."

"I expect it is," Win agreed.

"We were on opposite sides in that war," Randol said. "But, from the looks of things, we're on the same side in this one."

Win held out his hand. "Hold on," he said. "I didn't come here to fight in a war."

Randol chuckled. "You turned down Pendrake's offer to be one of his deputies, you've gone into business in competition with him, and you have announced publicly that you will not pay the sheriff's tax. You can't say you didn't come here to fight in a war, Mr. Coulter. Hell, you've started one."

Win smiled. "I reckon I can't argue with you on that," he said.

"You take care, Mr. Coulter," Randol said. "And, if

you need an ally you can count on me . . . and the power
of the press. And I promise you, I won't hide in the cellar
this time.''

Win stared at him for a long moment, then he put his
hand on the small editor's shoulder. ''About Lawrence?''

''Yes?''

''I'm glad you hid in the cellar,'' Win said.

8

As Win left the newspaper office, memories of Lawrence, Kansas, tumbled, unbidden, through his mind.

He and Joe walked down Lawrence's main street to move among the dead. They had seen this many dead before, especially after the battles they had participated in, where armed men were locked in desperate struggle against other armed men. But the dead here had not been killed in battle. They had been murdered in cold blood, in some cases, hauled out of their beds while still in their nightshirts and hacked to pieces, or shot down in front of their horrified families while their wives and children pleaded for their lives.

Among the victims were some very young boys, no more than nine or ten, and some very old men, including a few who Win was sure were eighty or more.

And, standing in the street, crying bitter tears over their loved ones, were the women of the town. By Quantrill's orders no woman had been molested, or physically injured. But Win knew that the pain inflicted upon these women's souls would never diminish, and he could feel the heart-chilling loathing in their stares.

At Quantrill's order the 400 men left Lawrence the same way they had entered it . . . at a gallop. When they reached the top of a hill about a mile out of town, Win stopped.

Twisting around in his saddle, he looked back toward the town. From here it looked as if the billowing, black smoke from over a hundred burning buildings had collected into one huge column to roil and surge into the sky. And though there was no sound, in Win's mind he could still hear the wailing sobs of the grieving wives, mothers, and daughters of the slain.

"What was the name of that town, again, Win?" Joe asked, stopping beside him to have the same vantage point.

"Lawrence," Win answered. "Lawrence, Kansas."

"Lawrence," Joe repeated. He was silent for a moment. "I want to remember it."

"Why?"

"Because," Joe explained, "I want to remember where it was that I left my soul."

Win was glad to hear that his brother was fighting the same devils he was. That meant that he wasn't alone.

CLEM BEALE, THE BARBER, GREETED HIM AS HE STEPPED through the front door of the "Elite Tonsorial Salon." The greeting had a salubrious effect on his mental well-being, by ridding him, at least temporarily, of the nightmarish memories of Lawrence.

"Good morning, Mr. Coulter," Beale said enthusiastically. "Welcome to my shop!"

"Good morning," Win replied. "Beale, isn't it?"

"Yes, sir! Clem Beale is the name, and barbering is the game." He laughed. "Catchy little rhyme, isn't it? Heard that when I was in Dallas, some time back. How's your brother?"

"My brother? He's fine, why do you ask?"

"Most of the town is still laughin' over the way he beat Deputy Reeves at his own game in poker last night. Then, when Reeves tried to make somethin' of it, why, your brother give him what for. Boxed his ears in real good, I hear. Ever'one agrees, Reeves has had somethin' like that comin' to him for a long time."

Win followed the barber into his shop, then settled into the lone chair. "Sometimes my brother gets a little riled up," he said.

"Yes, sir, well, Reeves has got lots of fellas riled up, I reckon. But, before your brother, no one ever had the guts to take him on." The barber held out his hand, palm up. "The shave and haircut will be four bits," he said. "Two bits for me, and two bits for the sheriff's tax."

Win took a half-dollar from his pocket and handed it to Beale. "Does every merchant in town collect Pendrake's tax, without complaint?" he asked.

Beale chuckled. "Well, sir, you're half right," he said. "Ever'one in town does collect the tax, but they don't do it without complaint. No, sir. 'Cause when you get right down to it, why, we have to pay that tax too, ever' time we visit someone else's place of business. But there's nothin' we can do about it."

"There's something I can do about it," Win said. "Starting today, anyone who buys a drink or a meal, or anything else in the Desert Flower, will not be charged a sheriff's tax."

"You don't say? How are you going to handle that? What are you going to say to Pendrake when he comes around for his money?"

"I'm not going to say anything," Win replied easily. "I'm just not going to pay him anything."

Beale put the fifty-cent piece in his cash box, then covered Win with a barber's cloth. "I sure wish you good luck," he said. He tipped Win back in the chair and started wrapping hot towels around his face.

"Luck has nothing to do with it," Win replied.

"Oh, would you like some lilac water?" the barber asked hopefully, holding up a bottle of green liquid. "Only five cents more . . . well, ten, with the sheriff's tax. And it'll make you smell real good."

"I smell good enough," Win said.

"Yes, sir, I'm sure you do," the barber answered, disappointed at losing the sale. He put the bottle back on the shelf, then started mixing up a lather.

At that moment a shadow fell across the room and when Win and the barber looked up, they saw Reeves standing in the door. Reeves was holding a pistol in his hand, pointing it toward the chair. With a little gasp of fear, Beale stepped quickly out of the way.

"I've heard about you, Coulter," Reeves said. "I've heard how you are plannin' on not chargin' anyone any tax when they come to your saloon. Is that right?"

"That's right," Win replied.

"You figurin' on cheatin' Pendrake out of his due, are you?"

"So, what if I am?" Win asked. "What do you care? You don't work for him anymore. He fired you."

"Yeah, because of you, he fired me. I had a good thing goin' till you came along to mess things up," Reeves said. He waved his gun around angrily. "You an' that no-count brother of yours."

"It could be that you had a better thing going than you deserved," Win said. "Maybe it was time someone came along to take that badge away from a mangy piece of dog shit like you."

"Yeah, well, I ain't goin' to be out of a job long," Reeves said. "Soon as I take you over to Pendrake and tell him how you ain't plannin' on payin' no taxes, he'll want me back."

"You think he hasn't heard that by now?" Win asked.

"Maybe he has heard it, but you're still walkin' around free. I aim to take care of that right now."

"Do you?"

"Yeah, I do. Now get up outta that chair." Again, he waved the pistol around.

"Reeves, I came here to get a shave and a haircut," Win said. "If I were you, I'd get out while I still could. Believe me, you don't want to get my dander up."

"What's that you say? I don't want to get your dander up?" Reeves said, as if unable to believe what he was hearing. "Why, you dumb son of a bitch! I'm the one holdin' the gun! If anybody is worried about gettin' dander up . . . you should be worryin' about me!''

"Mr. Reeves, why don't you just go along now?" Beale said. "I don't want any trouble in my barbershop."

"You stay the hell out of this, Beale," Reeves growled. He looked menacingly at Win. "That is, if you want to stay alive long enough to shave Coulter's dead ass."

"I'm giving you one more chance to walk away from this," Win said. "I'd suggest you take it."

"One more chance? One more chance? Mister, have you gone crazy?" Reeves asked, puzzled not only by Win's coolness but also by his strange remark.

"Walk out of here now and stay alive. Or push it further and die," Win said. "It's your choice."

Reeves laughed out loud. "Listen to him, will you, barber? I'm the one with the gun, and he's tellin' me I'm the one that's goin' to die."

The barber took the measure of the two men, then realized something that Reeves did not. There was not the slightest shadow of fear . . . or doubt . . . in Win's face. Reeves, on the other hand, even though he was the one holding a gun, seemed to be literally shaking with fright, so much so that it was all he could do to keep the gun steady.

"I've had enough of all this jawin'," Reeves said. "I aim to kill you right here an' right now, while you're a-sittin' in the barber's chair." Reeves's nostrils flared, his eyes narrowed, and a vein in his temple began to throb. Suddenly the little barbershop was filled with the sound of an exploding cartridge. The apron that had been spread across Win's body puffed up as a bullet tore through it . . . from the inside out. The shot left a tiny, brown ring of fire which blazed only for an instant, then went out.

After passing through the apron, the bullet hit Reeves in the chest, tore through his heart, then came out just above his left shoulder blade, leaving a quarter-sized exit wound. The impact of the heavy slug propelled Reeves back out through the door of the barbershop with such force that the door was torn from its hinges.

Though Reeves was already dead, the reflex action of his trigger finger caused his own pistol to discharge, firing harmlessly into the board sidewalk in front of the shop. Reeves fell back, faceup, off the edge of the sidewalk, landing with his head down in a freshly deposited pile of horse dung, while his legs were still up on the sidewalk itself. A spreading stain of blood soaked the front of his shirt.

Win stood up from the barber chair and pulled off the punctured apron. Still holding the smoking gun, he stepped outside to look down at Reeves's body. When he saw that Reeves was dead, he went back into the barbershop and sat again in the chair.

The sound of the two shots brought several people running to the barbershop. The first ones to arrive were the merely curious, shopkeepers and citizens. Amazingly, none of those who came were wearing badges. Apparently not even a gunshot could get any of the deputies out into the heat of midday.

One of the citizens who came hurrying toward the sprawled body was Doc Boyer. As he got close enough to see who it was, however, he slowed his pace, and by the time he got there he was moving at a leisurely walk. Without even bending over, he kicked at the sole of Reeves's boot.

"What about it, Doc?" someone asked.

"Doesn't take a medical degree to see that this one is dead," Doc said, and there was a nervous ripple of laughter.

"Who shot him?" someone asked.

"He was shot by Win Coulter," Clem Beale said. "Damnedest thing I ever seen in my life. Reeves here had his gun out and was pointin' it at Mr. Coulter. He was about to shoot him when, somehow, Mr. Coulter shot him first."

"Mr. Beale?" Win called from inside the barbershop.

"Yes, sir?" Beale replied, looking around, surprised that Win had gone back inside.

Win had already put the apron around himself and was leaning back in the reclining barber chair.

"What about that shave and haircut? Am I goin' to get it or not?" he asked.

"Yes, sir, shave and a haircut, comin' right up," Clem Beale said. But when the barber saw the brown-ringed hole in the apron and thought again of what had just happened right in front of him, he felt a cold fear come over him. A moment later, as he raised the razor to Win's jaw, his hand was shaking visibly. Win reached up to grab him by the wrist.

"I want my whiskers cut, not my throat," he said.

"Yes, sir," Beale said. He took a couple of deep breaths, forcing his hand to stop shaking. "Yes, sir," he said. "Your whiskers, not your throat."

9

HARLEY PENDRAKE STOOD AT THE FRONT DOOR OF THE sheriff's office, staring out at the town. Subdued winks of soft light shone from the windows of the houses back in the residential area, while the Gilded Cage and the Desert Flower spilled golden splashes of brightness onto the boardwalks. The street was noisy with piano playing, singing, drinking, and loud, raucous conversation.

The Desert Flower, Pendrake noticed, was every bit as busy tonight as was the Gilded Cage. The word on the street was that Win and Joe Coulter were not collecting the tax Pendrake had levied on every business in town.

"Boss, if that's true, and we don't do nothin' to stop them," one of his deputies said, "won't be long till ever' other business in town is goin' to be wantin' to do the same thing."

"Is that a fact?" Pendrake asked.

"Well, I mean, I was just thinkin' . . ."

"Don't think, Wallace," Pendrake said. "You ain't smart enough to think."

From the darkness of the street, came the sound of hollow hoofbeats as half a dozen drovers came riding into town.

"Sounds like a live town," a voice said from a distant spot.

"Yeah. Hope they got somethin' to eat in the saloon. I'm mighty tired of trail grub."

"Eat? Not me. I ain't goin' to have time to eat. I'm goin' to get so damned drunk I won't even know where I'm at."

"Hell, Johnny, most of the time you don't know where you're at anyhow," one of the others said.

All the drovers laughed, then rode on beyond Pendrake's earshot.

Behind Pendrake, in the sheriff's office, a few of his deputies were gathered. They were discussing the killing of Deputy Reeves this morning.

"It ain't right," one of them grumbled, just as Pendrake came back inside.

"What ain't right, Cummins?" Pendrake asked, putting a cheroot into his mouth, then leaning over to light it by the kerosene lantern.

"The way Reeves was shot down in the street," Deputy Cummins said. "I mean, the guy who shot him is still walkin' around, free as a bird. And Reeves was one of our'n."

Pendrake blew out a long puff of smoke, then stared at the deputy through narrow, obsidian eyes.

"He wasn't one of ours," Pendrake said. "I fired him this morning. He started that fight on his own."

"Still," Cummins grumbled. "It don't seem right to let the son of a bitch that shot him go."

"You want to settle scores for Reeves?" Pendrake asked.

"No, nothing like that. I was just . . ." Cummins let the sentence trail away, uncompleted.

"Look at you," Pendrake said. "In here, bitching and moaning because Reeves was dumb enough to get himself shot. I'll tell you this, and I'll tell it only one time. If Coulter hadn't killed Reeves this mornin', by tonight I likely would have. Reeves didn't have a pot to piss in, or a window to throw it out of, before I pinned a badge on him. Nor did any of you," he added. "All in the hell you men have to do is what I tell you to do. Nothing more, and nothing less. You do that, and we'll be all right."

"What about the fact that they ain't collecting taxes down at the Desert Flower?" Deputy Wallace asked.

"You let me worry about that," Pendrake replied. "All you men have to do is make certain everyone in town respects the law . . . my law," he added. "And if you can't make 'em respect it . . . then you damn well better make 'em fear it."

"How are we goin' to make 'em respect the law when the newspaper prints stuff like this?" one of the other deputies, a man named Cates, asked, holding up a copy of the day's newspaper. "Did you see this article? It's entitled, 'Is Our Reign of Terror Coming to an End?'"

Pendrake began reading the article.

Yet another shooting has taken place on the streets of what was once an industrious and productive town. Donald Reeves, one of the many deputies appointed by Sheriff Harley Pendrake, was shot down in front of the barbershop this morning by one Win Coulter.

According to an eyewitness who does not wish to be identified, Mr. Coulter came into the barbershop for the legal and peaceful purpose of seeking a haircut and a shave. He was accosted by Reeves, shortly after taking his seat in the barber chair.

"I have heard about you, Coulter," Reeves is reported to have said. "I have heard that it is your intention not to charge your customers the rightfully assessed tax. Is my source correct?"

"It is, sir," Mr. Coulter replied.

"By acting in such unaccord with the law, you are denying Sheriff Pendrake his just due," Reeves continued, speaking of that accursed tax which has placed such an unfair burden upon all the good citizens of this beleaguered city.

"If so, why should you care?" Coulter responded,

reminding the erstwhile deputy that he was no longer
in a position of authority.

At this reminder, Mr. Reeves became extremely
agitated. It was then, it is reported, that he began to
wave his gun around angrily.

"Perhaps you had a better position than you deserved," Coulter suggested.

Reeves then replied that he did not intend to be
unemployed for very long, stating his belief that if he
collected the tax due the sheriff he would, surely, be
reinstated, whereupon he ordered Coulter to get up
from the barber's chair, emphasizing his order with
the showing of his pistol.

"Reeves, I came here to get a shave and a haircut," Coulter said, clearly trying to defuse the situation. "If I were you, I would get out while I still
could. Believe me, you don't want to get my dander
up."

At that suggestion, Mr. Reeves is reported to have
grown even more belligerent, stating that if there was
cause for worry it should be Coulter worrying about
upsetting him. The cause for Mr. Reeves's confidence
was the fact that he was clearly displaying a pistol,
whereas Mr. Coulter was still seated in the barber's
chair.

Clem Beale, the barber, then made his own appeal
for Deputy Reeves to leave his establishment in
peace, but again Reeves refused to go, apparently intent upon perpetrating violence, regardless of the genuine efforts of both Mr. Coulter and Mr. Beale to
defuse the situation.

What further words were spoken, if indeed any
were, have now been lost in the tumult of events.
What is known in that Deputy Reeves was holding a
.44 caliber engine of death, and when his thumb
pulled back upon the hammer of the pistol, it was a
fair indication, had one been needed, that he had
every intention of activating the weapon.

Whereupon, our unnamed eyewitness reports, the

interior of his tonsorial establishment was filled with the noise of exploding gunpowder. The ball thus energized, however, did not come from Mr. Reeves's pistol, but from a weapon that was discharged from beneath the barber's apron, it having never left Mr. Coulter's possession, even as he prepared for a shave and a haircut.

While the death of any human being is a somber event, there are, nevertheless, times when such an occasion is necessary. Legal hangings of desperadoes are one such example. The death of Donald Reeves is another, for the good citizens of this town well know that it was his bullet which ended the life of Parson Rockwall for no more reason than the playing out of an irresponsible bet.

Although he is not singularly responsible for all the evil which has so recently befallen us, Reeves, as one of Pendrake's deputies, was clearly representative of all that is wrong with our fair town. This writer feels reasonably certain in making the statement that there are none who will mourn his passing.

While it may have been a bullet fired from Win Coulter's pistol which dispatched Donald Reeves to his appointed rendezvous with the devil himself, in so doing, Win Coulter was, this writer feels, but the instrument of justice.

"Listen, Sheriff, we can't let that son of a bitch go on publishing stories like that," Cates said when he saw that Pendrake was finished reading. "That's the kind of thing that can get people riled up enough to do somethin'."

"You don't worry about Randol."

"I could pay a visit to him now, if you want," Cates suggested.

Pendrake stroked his chin as he contemplated the offer for a moment. "No," he finally said. "No, not yet. First things first. Right now we have to make certain we ain't losin' control of this town."

● ● ●

At the same time, down at the far end of the street in a restaurant called Helga's, Doc had invited Win and Joe to join him for supper. Helga herself came over to the table to take their order. She was a tall, strapping woman in her late twenties. Her blond hair was tied back in a bun, but an errant strand had fallen across her bright blue eyes, and when she pushed it back, she left a smudge of flour on her cheek. Her eyes shone brightly as she looked at Joe.

"*Ja*, do you want something for to eat?" she asked.

Joe ordered.

"Some biscuits, maybe half a dozen, fried taters, maybe a mess of fried onions, and a couple of steaks. You got any pie?"

"*Ja*, cherry and apple I have," Helga said.

"I'll have a slice of each," Joe said.

Helga smiled. "*Ist gut* to see a man that eats a *gut* supper," she said.

"Supper?" Win chuckled. "Ma'am, he won't be eatin' his supper till about eleven tonight. This is just to tide himself over."

Helga took the other orders, then left the dining room. Doc saw Joe's eyes follow her all the way to the kitchen.

"She's a nice lady," Doc said.

"I was just thinking that myself," Joe replied. "How come she talks like that?"

"She's German," Doc answered. "She came to America as a mail-order bride to marry some little weasel of a storekeeper. When she got off the stage and he saw how much bigger than him she was, he packed up and left town."

"You mean he run out on her?"

"That's what happened all right. And poor Helga had used just about ever' cent she had in the world just to get over here. When he left town Helga was broke with no place to go."

"What did she do?"

"She got a job cooking over at the Gilded Cage. But when Pendrake bought the Gilded Cage he said any woman who worked for him would also have to whore for him. Helga wouldn't whore, so she put what little money she had saved into this place and opened her own restaurant.''

"Looks like she's doin' all right," Win said.

"She could do better if Pendrake wasn't bleeding her to death with his taxes. Course, he's doing that to everyone else as well, so she's not alone.''

"Tell me a little more about Pendrake," Win said. "He obviously has everyone in town buffaloed. Just how fast is he with that gun of his?''

Doc took a swallow of his coffee.

"Fast? Well, I don't know. I can't really comment on how fast he is. You can only judge that by men you have seen in gunfights. Pendrake doesn't have gunfights . . . he just kills people. He can shoot a man in the back as easily as he can swat a fly. As near as I can tell, he has no sense of human feeling whatever . . . no hate, no love, no fear, no interest in women, no interest in whiskey, nothing. Killing is as easy for him as sneezing.''

"He must have an interest in money," Win said.

"I suppose he does. He's sucking the town dry, that's for sure," Doc said. "But to be honest with you, I don't know if that is as much an interest in money as it is in just watching the town grovel before him.''

Helga brought their food then, and as Win ate his supper he contemplated what Doc had just told him. Fast gunfighters, men who sold their speed, were a predictable breed. Even the worst of them had the common denominator of pride to drive them. Sometimes an opponent could use that pride to his advantage.

It was the cold-blooded killers like Pendrake, who had nothing in common with other men, who were the most dangerous. Win had learned that during the war. He had seen men like Quantrill and Bloody Bill Anderson, and even Jesse James, kill without compunction. He knew such men, even if he didn't fully understand them.

IT WAS CROWDED IN THE GILDED CAGE. AT ONE TABLE were the six cowboys who had ridden into town earlier in the evening. They were going back south after a drive, but now they were playing cards and getting drunk on cheap whiskey. A cloud of noxious smoke from the strong "roll your owns" they were smoking hovered over the table. The men were playing poker and unwinding from a long and difficult period on the trail. For them, unwinding meant drinking, and the whiskey had not only relaxed them, it had made them quite boisterous. Their presence had been made known to the others in the saloon from the moment they arrived. They laughed uproariously at each other's jokes and comments, celebrated victorious hands, and lamented the poor ones.

"All right, boys, we're down to the nut-cutting," one of the players said. "What you got?"

"I got me two pair, kings and sevens," one of the players said hopefully.

All but one of the other players had lesser hands. But one had a full house, and he let out a happy whoop, then got up and started doing a little dance. His spurs tangled and he fell flat on his back.

"Hey, Jed, iffen your back's too bad hurt, I'll take your winnin's and go get a whore for you," one of the others said amidst the laughter.

"Hurt? You think I'm hurt?" Jed shouted. He hopped up. "Give me your hat. I'll show you I ain't hurt. I'm goin' to do me a Mexican hat dance."

Jed grabbed a hat and started dancing around it. But, as before, he got his spurs tangled and tripped, only this time instead of falling to the floor, he fell against another table. There were four men at the table, all of them wearing deputies' badges.

"Get away from me, you drunken bastard!" Deputy Burke shouted, pushing Jed away.

"Hell, mister, you don't have to get your dander up over it," Jed replied. "I was just funnin' is all."

"You're drunk and disturbin' the peace, every one of you," the deputy said. "Come on, you're under arrest. All of you."

The laughter stopped.

"Did you hear what I said? You are all goin' to jail."

Jed shook his head, and held out his hand, as if holding

Burke away from him. "No, sir, we ain't goin' to jail," he said. "Frank, you go over there and pick up Johnny." Johnny, the youngest of their number, was sitting at the same table with them, but, unable to hold his whiskey, he was already passed out. "Come on, boys, if our company and our money ain't appreciated around here, we'll just leave this place."

The four deputies stood up.

"You're goin' to jail," Burke said again.

"No, sir. We ain't goin' to no goddamn jail. Not for doin' nothin' no more'n a little funnin'. I told you, we'll get out of here so's we ain't disturbin' no one anymore. That's goin' to have to be enough for you, 'cause we ain't goin' to jail. Come on, boys, we'll just back out of here, slow and easy-like."

Jed started over to pick up Johnny as the others began moving toward the door. At that moment the four deputies suddenly drew on them.

"No, mister! Don't do that!" Jed shouted, and, seeing what was happening, the cowboys had no choice but to draw their own guns. Both sides opened fire, and for a moment the room was alive with the flash and crash of gunfire. When the cloud of gun smoke drifted away, two of the cowboys were lying dead on the floor, along with two of the deputies. The remaining deputies were gone, having fled through the back door.

"Oh, Jesus!" Jed said. "Mills, Austin, are you boys dead? Look at them, Frank."

"Mills and Austin is dead," Frank reported. "Wes is hurt."

"How bad?"

"Jesus," Wes said, his voice strained with pain as he sat down heavily in a nearby chair. Blood was oozing through the fingers of the hand he was holding over a wound in his stomach. "It hurts, Jed. Oh, sweet Jesus, it hurts."

"My God!" Jed said. "All we wanted to do was to drink a little whiskey and play some cards." He looked over toward the bartender, then toward the other patrons, who were now looking on in wide-eyed shock and dead silence.

"We didn't want this! We didn't want nothin' like this! How come you folks didn't do nothin' to stop it?"

"Do something, Jed. You gotta help me," Wes said. "I'm hurtin' awful bad."

"Frank, you help Wes," Jed said. "I'll get Johnny." Johnny was still passed out at the table, unhit by any of the bullets and blissfully unaware of what had just transpired. "We got to get out of here."

"What about Mills and Austin?"

Jed shook his head. "I hate leavin' 'em here, but we got no choice. Them deputies is crazy! We got to get out of here!"

Suddenly the batwing doors to the saloon swung open and half a dozen deputies came rushing in, all carrying shotguns. The two deputies who had disappeared earlier were with them.

"That's them!" Burke shouted, pointing to Jed and his friends. "They're the ones who started the fight. They murdered Cates and Everly."

"What?" Jed replied. "What are you talkin' about, mister? We didn't start no fight, and we didn't murder nobody. You started shootin' first. We shot back in self-defense."

"I say you murdered Cates and Everly," Burke repeated.

"What about our pards, Mills and Austin? They're dead too," Jed insisted.

"Come on, let's take 'em to Pendrake."

"A HANGIN'!" SOMEONE SHOUTED A FEW MINUTES LATER, rushing into the dining room at Helga's Cafe to spread the news. "They's goin' to be a hangin'."

The news fell like a bombshell. Within seconds of the announcement, everyone in the dining room was rushing for the door.

"What's going on? Is there going to be a lynching?" Win asked.

"Same as a lynching," Doc said. "Though, like as not, it's what Pendrake calls a legal hanging. That is, it'll be legal after he holds court."

"And when will that be?"

"Right now," Doc said. "The one thing Pendrake does believe in is giving everyone a speedy trial."

"How is it that Pendrake is both the sheriff and the judge?" Win asked.

Doc snorted. "The town made him a sheriff, the governor made him a judge. We're just lucky, I guess."

"Come on, Win, I missed my own trial," Joe said. "Let's see what this is all about. I'd sort of like to see how this fella operates."

When Win, Joe, and Doc reached the street, they saw half a dozen mounted men. Behind them, hog-tied so that they couldn't even stand, were four more men. They were being dragged behind the horses, through the dirt and manure piles in the street. One of the four was badly wounded, another was passed out. The two who were conscious and unhurt were shouting and cursing angrily.

"Let us go, goddamn it! Who the hell are you, anyway?"

The commotion had drawn more people than just the curious from Helga's Cafe. They were coming from all over town. Saloons and stores were emptying as the good citizens, drawn by the powerful seduction of instant death, poured into the street. Except for the spill of light from the buildings, it was very dark, but a couple of men had lit torches and were carrying them as they followed the crowd. The four men were dragged for the entire length of the street, until they reached the front of the sheriff's office.

Pendrake was standing on the front porch of the sheriff's office, casually smoking a cigar. When the four cowboys were deposited in front of him, he stepped out to the front of the porch and looked down at them.

"These the prisoners?" Pendrake asked.

"Yeah, Sheriff, I mean, Your Honor," Burke said, changing forms of address to suit the occasion. "This is them," Burke said.

"What are they being charged with?"

"Murder, Your Honor. They killed Cates and Everly."

Pendrake took the cigar out of his mouth, then looked out over the crowd gathered in the street.

"Citizens of Belle Springs!" he shouted to them. "I call this court into session!"

"Court?" someone shouted from the crowd. "You have the audacity to call this a court?"

"Who is that brave man?" Joe asked.

"I met him today," Win replied. "His name is Ed Randol. He is the newspaperman."

"This is a court if I say it's a court, Randol," Pendrake replied. "And all the writin' in that lyin' rag of a newspaper of yours ain't gonna change things. Deputy Burke, get these here prisoners on their feet. This is a court of law and they got to show some respect."

"They's only two of 'em can stand, Sheriff," Burke replied. "One of 'em's too bad shot up and the other'n is passed out drunk."

"Very well, then get the two who can stand onto their feet."

Jed and Frank were forced to stand. Wes and Johnny remained lying in the dirt.

"Deputy Burke, you were in the saloon when this happened?" Pendrake asked.

"I was."

"Take a good look at these here men and tell me if they was the ones who killed Cates and Everly."

"They was the ones," Burke said without moving from his position.

"Goddamn it, I said take a good look," Pendrake ordered. "This here court is goin' to be fair. Put a torch in front of 'em so's you can see 'em good."

One of the torchbearers held his light in front of the prisoners. By the wavering gold light of the fire, Win could see the look of terror in the faces of the cowboys.

"Yes, sir, Sheriff, that was them. We tried to arrest them for bein' drunk and disturbin' the peace. That's when they pulled their guns on us and started shootin'."

"You're a lyin' son of a bitch!" Jed shouted. "That ain't true and you damn well know it. We was leavin' peaceful-like. You started shootin' first, and we had no choice but to defend ourselves."

"What's your name?" Pendrake asked.

"Jed Summers."

"You admit you done the shootin'?"

"Yeah, we done the shootin', but, like I said, we was just defendin' ourselves."

"Before the shooting began, did the deputies try and arrest you?"

"We wasn't doin' nothin'."

"Did the deputies try and arrest you?"

"Yeah."

"You do realize, don't you, that if you had submitted to arrest, none of this would have happened?" Pendrake said. "Cates and Everly would be alive, your two friends would be alive, that one wouldn't be hurt."

"All that happened when the deputies commenced shootin'," Jed said.

"Regardless of who began shootin' first, you was put under arrest and you refused to go. That bein' the case, Mr. Summers, you stand convicted by your own words. There can be no claim of self-defense when you brutally shoot down an officer of the law what was only doin' his duty. I find you all guilty of murder, and sentence all of you to hang."

"What about the one that was drunk?" one of the deputies asked. "We goin' to hang him too?"

"Hang him too," Pendrake said. "In my court, justice will be done."

"Court?" Jed shouted. "This ain't no court! This is a city street. And justice? This ain't justice. This here is a lynchin'. You hang us, you'll be doin' murder."

"Take them to the place of execution," Pendrake said by way of dismissal.

"Damn, Win, looks like they're actually goin' to hang them men," Joe said.

"Looks like," Win agreed.

"Well, we just goin' to stand here and not do anything?"

"You have any ideas about what we can do?" Win asked.

"No," Joe admitted. "But seems to me like we ought to be able to do somethin'."

At that moment, Burke backed a buckboard under a large elm tree that stood in front of the livery stable, which was just across the street from the sheriff's office. Immediately thereafter, someone tossed four ropes over a big limb that ran at right angles to the tree trunk about fifteen feet above the ground.

"Get the prisoners onto the gallows," Pendrake ordered.

"Hey," one of the deputies called. He was standing over Wes. "This here'n has died."

"Don't matter none," Pendrake replied. "He's been sentenced to hang, he's goin' to hang. Get him up there with the others."

Jed and Frank were dragged over to the buckboard, lifted up onto it, then had ropes put around their necks. Next the deputies lifted up Wes's body and connected it. Finally they slipped a noose around Johnny's neck, pulling him to his feet by the pressure of the rope.

Johnny, who had been completely out of it until now, began gagging and choking. He opened his eyes and looked around, not understanding where he was or what was happening to him.

"You men got anything to say?" Pendrake asked. "Any messages for your family back home?"

"Jed?" Johnny asked in a small, frightened voice. Jed was the oldest, and the natural leader of the bunch. "Jed, what's goin' on?"

"We're about to get ourselves hung, Johnny," Jed said.

"What are you talkin' about? My God! Jed!" Johnny started screaming, and Pendrake pointed to him.

"Put a gag in that fella's mouth," he ordered.

A rag was stuffed in Johnny's mouth, then a handkerchief tied around to keep it in. Johnny's screams quieted, and he looked on at the proceedings with eyes wide in terror and confusion.

"Jed . . . Jed, goddamn . . . they're really goin' to go through with it!" Frank said.

"Take it easy, Frank," Jed said. "Buck up and be a man

about it. Don't let these sons of bitches see us afraid.''

"What about a preacher?'' Frank asked. "Don't we get no preacher?''

"Yeah, Pendrake, how about it?'' Randol shouted. "Oh, yes, that's right. You can't give a preacher because one of your deputies killed our preacher.''

"Justice has been served in that case, Randol. Reeves is the one who killed the preacher, and Reeves is now dead . . . as you well know.''

"That's true, but you sure didn't have anything to do with it,'' Randol accused.

"I'm sorry, boys, but there ain't no preacher,'' Pendrake said. "I'll give you a moment to make your peace.''

"Oh . . . my God!'' Frank shouted.

"Frank, Johnny, hold on, boys, we're about to take us one hell of a trip. We'll meet on the other side,'' Jed said.

Pendrake turned to address the crowd. "Let this here hangin' be a lesson to ever'one!'' he shouted. "There is law in Belle Springs! And the law . . . all laws, includin' the laws about taxes,'' he added pointedly, "will be enforced.'' He turned to Burke, who was still sitting quietly on the seat of the buckboard. "Deputy Burke, carry out the sentence.''

Burke snapped the reins, and the team jerked the buckboard forward. The four cowboys were pulled off the back of the little wagon, then they hung from the tree. Johnny and Wes hung easily, moving back and forth in a slow arc caused by the pull of the wagon. But Jed and Frank weren't as fortunate. They were slowly strangling, lifting their legs and bending at the waist as if in such a way they could take some of the pressure off their necks.

There was a wail of sympathy and indignation from the crowd, but every man present stood glued to the scene by morbid curiosity.

Win stared directly at Pendrake. Pendrake was calmly relighting his cigar. Then he turned and went back into his office, without so much as a backward glance at the four bodies, hanging from the tree.

10

THE TOWN OF BELLE SPRINGS, SO WILD AND NOISY THE night before, was relatively quiet this morning. Win and Joe stood on the plank walk in front of the Desert Flower and looked down Main Street at the town.

At the far end of the street the mortician's wagon was pulled up under the hanging tree. The four young cowboys had hung from the tree all night, and now Parker Luscomb, the undertaker, a tall, cadaverous man dressed all in black with a high hat, had come to claim his prize. Luscomb stood beside his wagon watching, occasionally raising a thin arm to point with a bony finger as he gave directions to his grave digger. The grave digger was a strongly built man, who was cutting down the four cowboys.

He took down the last one. This was the cowboy who had been wounded in the gunfight, and his chest was covered by blood, dried now to a reddish brown. His body was laid out in the wagon with the other three. From there they would be taken to the hardware store where a back room served as the mortuary.

"What I don't understand," Win said, "is why the folks

in this town stay around and put up with all this. Why don't
they just move away?''

"This is where they were making their home," Joe answered. "It's hard to just pull up stakes and leave like
that.''

Win thought of their farm back in Missouri, the farm
that had been burned to the ground by Kansas Jayhawkers
during the war. His and Joe's parents had been killed in
the same raid, and their bodies burned with the house. He
ran his hand through his hair.

"Yeah," he said gruffly. He spit. "Yeah, I guess I know
what you mean.''

Win knew exactly what was going through his brother's
mind at that moment. In Win's heart, he knew that he
would have never stayed on the farm. But Joe had loved
the land, loved farming, and had not felt completely whole
since that terrible tragedy.

Win put his hand out to squeeze his brother's shoulder.

"You all right, Little Brother?" he asked quietly.

"Yeah, Win, I'm all right," Joe answered. "Listen, I
think I'll go back in here and have some breakfast. You
want to come with me?''

Win looked at his brother in surprise. "We had a biscuit
and a cup of coffee. I thought that was breakfast.''

Joe smiled. "That sure ain't no breakfast for a working
man," he said. "Come on, what do you say?''

"You go ahead and enjoy your breakfast, Joe," Win
said. "I think I'll take a walk around town.''

"Be careful," Joe warned, as he disappeared back inside
the saloon.

Win nodded, then started walking. Maybe Joe could understand why someone wouldn't want to leave, but Win
couldn't. What was there about this town that was worth
saving? He certainly had no intentions of hanging on to the
saloon for any length of time, though he would have to
make certain that it was worth something if he was going
to get anything out of it. And if the town didn't make it,
then neither would his saloon. Viewed in such a way, Win
realized that he had a vested interest in the town's survival.

That being the case, he looked over the town with renewed curiosity.

The street he was on, Main Street, ran north and south. In the relatively short distance between where he was standing and the railroad at the far end of town, Main was intersected by two streets: First and Second.

First and Second streets consisted only of residences, and though they started out, boldly, as streets . . . they faded away rather quickly into barely discernable trails at each end.

All of the business establishments were on Main Street on this side of the tracks, or on Third Street, which formed the cross of a "T" on the other side of the tracks.

At the head of Main Street stood a white-frame church. The sign out front identified it as a Methodist Church. A black wreath on the door denoted the recent passing of the church's parson. The first business establishment on the east side of the street at the extreme north end of town was the Desert Flower. Next came the Morning Star Hotel, which had a dining room, then Helga's Cafe. Because the Desert Flower also served food, that meant that there were three eating establishments located side by side. As a result, the town's residents, when they could still smile, referred to this corner of town as "Bean Corner."

Once you crossed First Street and continued south were the feed store, Ling Lee's laundry, and the newspaper office. On the southeast corner of Second Street there was the hardware store with an exposed stairway climbing up the side, leading up to the doc's office. The last establishment before reaching the railroad was the barbershop.

On the west side of the street, starting at the north end, was the bank, the general store, then the leather goods store. Across First Street was a gunsmith shop, an apothecary, then the Gilded Cage saloon. Second Street separated the Gilded Cage from the jail. In an open lot between the jail and the railroad stood the cottonwood tree from which the four young cowboys had been hanged last night.

At the south end of Main Street, and running at right angles to it, was the GSR, or the Great Southwest Railroad.

On the other side of the tracks sat the depot building. Behind the depot, also running east and west, was Third Street. The livery stable and corral, the blacksmith's shop, and the meat market were all on Third Street. Also on Third Street was the Roman Catholic church, an old, stone Spanish mission that had stood in that same spot for nearly 100 years before the rest of the town was ever born. Beyond Third Street, about half a mile up a winding road, was the copper smelter. With its huge ore chute and towering smokestacks, it dominated the town, even though it was, technically, beyond the town limits.

Climbing up the denuded mountain behind the smelter was a filigree of flumes and scaffolding, dotted here and there with the scar of a mine opening, going deep into the bowels of the dark, granite slab that was Mount Carlisle.

As Win walked down the street, he heard a loud crashing noise in the building just in front of him. A large box came flying through the door, landed in the street, then broke open and scattered its contents in the dirt. Ed Randol, the publisher, wearing an ink-stained apron, ran out of the newspaper office into the street and knelt in the dirt to begin picking up the scattered type.

"Just leave it there, Randol!" a gruff voice called. Burke, Wallace, and Logan came out of the newspaper office then.

"Burke, Wallace, Logan, I know all of you," Randol said. He pointed to them. "What you are doing is interfering with the rights of a free press. That is a violation of the Constitution."

"No, I'll tell you what is a violation. It's the trash you're printin' in this rag you're callin' a newspaper," Burke said. "Why, this is even worse'n what you did yesterday. Sheriff Pendrake is a patient man, but he ain't gonna put up with this." Burke held a wadded-up page in his hand.

"Every word is the truth," Randol insisted. "Those men were hanged without a trial."

"They had a trial."

"That was a mockery of justice."

"Well, that's just too bad then, ain't it? 'Cause that's the only justice there is around here," Burke snarled. He kicked the box, scattering the type for a second time. Randol started picking it up.

"I said leave it!" Burke said. He had his pistol out and pointing at Randol. Randol stood up, shaking with fear and rage.

"Look at him shake, Burke," Deputy Wallace said, laughing. "You ever see a fella shake like that?"

"Looks to me like he's about to pee in his pants," Logan added.

"Haw! Wouldn't that be a sight, now?" Burke asked.

"Please," Randol said to the few who had gathered around to watch. "Someone help me." He saw Win. "You! You're the one I wrote about in my editorial yesterday. You aren't afraid of these people. Please help me."

"You plannin' on gettin' involved in this, mister?" Burke asked.

Win held out his hand. "No," he said pointedly. "This ain't none of my business."

Burke smiled broadly. "Well, now, I'm glad to see you're comin' to your senses. I reckon you'll be puttin' on a badge and comin' over to our side now."

Win didn't answer.

"Well?" Burke asked. "You are comin' over to our side, ain't you?"

"He didn't say he was on our side, Burke," Wallace said. "He said it weren't none of his business."

"The way I look at it," Burke went on. "He's either for us, or agin us. Right, mister?"

By now a dozen onlookers had gathered to watch, and twice as many people were being drawn to the scene, hurrying down the boardwalk, rushing across the street, spilling out of the stores and business establishments.

Win started to walk away.

"Hey, you! Don't you walk away from me like that!" Burke challenged, calling after him. "I asked you a question. You ain't answered me yet."

"Let it be, Deputy," Win said.

The smile left Burke's face. "Maybe you ain't gettin'

the whole picture here. Now, if you want to be friendly, answer the question.''

Win continued to walk away.

''Mister! Are you lookin' to die?''

Win stopped and sighed. It had gone the limit now . . . he knew a killing was about to take place. He felt no hot rush of blood, no fear. He felt only a deadly calm and an absolute assurance that he would come out on top.

He turned around, slowly.

Burke grinned broadly. ''Well, now, I was wonderin' what it would take to get through to you.''

Win looked down at the street, at the type still scattered in the dirt, then he looked back at Burke. Burke was still smiling, cocksure of himself.

''Your name is Burke?''

''Yeah.''

''Burke, pick up this man's type,'' Win ordered quietly.

The crowd of onlookers was large now, and there was a collective gasp as they realized what Win said.

Burke laughed a short, ugly laugh.

''What did you say?''

''I told you to pick up this man's type.''

''Mister, you talk like you just took leave of your senses,'' Burke said.

''You tell 'im, Burke,'' Wallace said.

''I ain't goin' to tell you again,'' Win said. ''Pick up the type.''

''Now, why the hell would I want to do such a thing?'' Burke asked.

''Because, if you don't, I'll kill you where you stand.''

Again, there was a collective gasp of surprise, for while Win's gun was still in its holster, Burke was holding his.

''What the hell, mister, you tryin' to commit suicide or somethin'? You do see that I have my gun out, don't you?'' Burke asked. ''And I ain't as stupid as Reeves was. He braced you when you was holdin' a gun underneath the barber's apron. You ain't got no apron coverin' you now.''

Win said nothing.

''I mean . . . suppose I just decided to shoot this newspaper fella and put him out of his misery?'' Burke suggested. ''There wouldn't be nothin' you could do about it.''

''No, I reckon not,'' Win said easily. ''Go ahead, shoot him.''

There was another collective gasp from the crowd.

''What'd you say?'' Burke asked.

''I said shoot him. Hell, he doesn't mean anything to me.''

''You . . . you want me to shoot him?'' Burke asked, surprised by Win's comment.

''Either shoot him, or quit talking about it,'' Win said.

''You're bluffin'. You think I won't shoot him.''

''He's likely to get shot anyway when the killin' starts.''

Burke blinked. ''The killin'?''

Win snorted. ''You'll be dead, the newspaperman will be dead, and at least one of the two deputies will be.''

Win looked at the two deputies. The expressions on their faces showed that they were not nearly as confident as they had been a moment earlier, and yet nothing had changed. Their man still had his pistol in his hand; Win's pistol was still in his holster.

But there was something about Win's voice, something cold and dry, like the rattling of bones in a graveyard. Despite himself, Burke felt a quick stab of fire shoot through him.

''And what about you? You'll be dead too,'' Burke said.

Win nodded. ''More'n likely I will be.''

''And it don't mean nothin' to you?''

''Not a damn thing,'' Win replied.

''You . . . you are crazy,'' Burke said.

''Shoot the newspaperman now, and let's get the killin' started,'' Win said coldly.

''Never mind the newspaperman!'' Wallace shouted nervously. ''Shoot this son of a bitch! You got the gun in your hand! Shoot 'im!''

Burke forced himself to smile, then he started to come back on the hammer of his pistol, all the while moving it around to bring it to bear on Win. He didn't even get it half-cocked before Win had his Colt in his hand. There was a snap of primer cap, then a roar of exploding powder, though both events happened so quickly as to be one loud bang. A finger of flame shot from the end of Win's Colt. Burke dropped his pistol and grabbed his chest. His eyes opened wide in pain and shock. He fell against the doorjamb of the newspaper office, then slid down to the sidewalk, leaving a smear of blood on the wall behind him. He wound up in the sitting position, his eyes open and blank.

"My God, did you see that?" someone in the crowd asked. "This feller just kilt Burke, with Burke holdin' a gun in his hand."

"I ain't never seen anyone that fast."

Win looked at the other two deputies. Neither of them had drawn, having felt secure in the fact that Burke already had his pistol out.

Shooting Burke had been easy, but only someone with Win's experience would realize that. Win had looked deep into Burke's eyes and knew he would stop and think before he actually pulled the trigger of his pistol. While he was thinking about it, Win would be acting, and drawing and shooting for someone with Win's speed was one step, not two.

"Pick up the type," Win ordered coldly.

"Yes, sir," one of the two remaining deputies mumbled.

As the two deputies scrambled to pick up the type, Win put his gun back in his holster and walked away. He could feel the two deputies' eyes boring holes in his back, but he didn't bother to look around. He knew they would be too afraid to draw.

LATER THAT SAME AFTERNOON, DEPUTY JESSUP CUMMINS was sitting at the desk in the sheriff's office. Pendrake was next door in the Gilded Cage, with Deputy Arnie Logan. Jessup Cummins and Larry Wallace were to, in the words of Pendrake, "keep their eyes on things."

Wallace was lying on a bunk in the nearest cell. He wasn't asleep, though his hat was pulled down over his eyes.

"You sleepin' in there, Wallace, leavin' me to do all the work?" Cummins asked.

"What work?" Wallace replied.

"Hell, you heard what Pendrake told us. He said we was to keep an eye on things. How you goin' to keep an eye on things if they're both shut and covered with that hat?"

"You do it for me."

Cummins chuckled. "Like I said, you're leavin' me to do all the work."

"I been thinkin'," Wallace said.

"Knowin' you, that's hard enough work," Cummins answered. "What you been thinkin' about?"

"'Pears like we're gettin' our numbers whittled down right good. I mean first it was Deputy Reeves who got killed, then Everly and Cates, then Burke."

"It don't bother me none," Cummins replied. "The way I look at it, the fewer of us there are, the bigger the piece of the pie."

"It don't bother you none, huh? Well, that's 'cause you didn't see that Coulter fella in action. I did."

"He was lucky, that's all," Cummins said. "They's nobody so good he can do what you said he done . . . not without he had some luck."

"No, he wasn't lucky. He was good," Wallace said. "He is the best I ever seen."

"That's because you've never seen the best," a low, hissing voice said.

Neither Cummins nor Wallace had heard the man come in. Startled, Wallace sat up on the bunk in the cell and found himself looking at the whitest man he had ever seen. The man's skin and hair were without color, and his eyes were a pale pink.

"My God, who are you?" Cummins asked.

"The name is Black . . . George Black."

"Black?" Wallace said. He laughed out loud and pointed. "Your name is Black?"

"Yes," Black said. "What is so funny about my name?"

"Well, I mean . . . can't you see the . . ." Wallace started, then, seeing that the albino had no sense of humor whatever, the laughter died in his throat. "Never mind. What, uh, can we do for you, Mr. Black?"

"I'm here to see Pendrake."

"He's not here right now, he's—"

"You. Go get him," Black said to Cummins.

"Now, hold on here! Who do you think you are, ordering me . . ." Cummins started, then, as with Wallace before, the comment went unfinished. There was something about this man that generated a primordial sense of fear. Looking into those cold, pink eyes, Cummins could almost believe he was looking into his own grave. He cleared his throat. "All right," he said. "You wait here, I'll get him for you."

"THE ALBINO IS HERE?" PENDRAKE SAID WHEN CUMMINS took him the message. "Good, I was hoping he would come. I sent for him, but I wasn't sure."

"Sheriff, do you know this man?"

"Yes, I know him. I knew him back in West Texas."

"He's a . . . strange sort of duck, isn't he?"

"He's an albino."

Cummins shook his head. "No," he said. "No, I don't mean that."

"Then what do you mean?"

"I don't know," Cummins admitted. "I don't know what I mean. I only know that I don't intend to spend much time around him."

11

CLAIRE WAS SITTING AT A TABLE IN A SMALL ROOM AT the back of the saloon, drinking coffee, when Win came in.

"Evenin'," Win said. Seeing the coffeepot on the stove, he asked, "Mind if I pour myself a cup of coffee and join you?"

Claire smiled at him. "You'd be welcome company," she said.

Win poured himself a cup, then sat down across from her. He took a drink, slurping the coffee through extended lips to keep from burning them.

"Did they get those poor boys buried?" Claire asked.

"Yes."

"Those poor boys, buried here in a strange graveyard in a strange town, their fate unknown to anyone who knew or loved them."

"Every man who ever goes on the trail faces that possibility," Win said. "Take Joe or me. One or both of us could be lyin' in a grave anywhere between here and Missouri. That's the fate of the wandering man."

"Yes, but you're not a wandering man anymore," Claire said.

Win took another swallow of his coffee and stared at her over the cup. ''Why do you think that?''

''Well, you're here now, and you're a property owner,'' she said. ''Surely you'll stay.''

''I'll stay until the Desert Flower is on its feet again,'' he said. ''Then I intend to sell out.''

''Sell out? To who?''

''I thought maybe to Harry,'' Win said. He paused for a moment. ''And to you,'' he added.

''To me?''

''If you would be interested.''

Claire drummed her fingers on the table for a moment or two, then she nodded. ''Yes,'' she said. ''Yes, I just might be. Although, without you, I don't see how we can make a go of it. Not as long as Pendrake is running the town.''

''I have a feeling things won't be going his way too much longer,'' Win said.

''Why do you think that?''

''When the others in town see that we don't intend to pay his tax, they'll stop paying him as well. And if a few more stop, then a few more, it will spread until the entire town revolts.''

Claire shook her head. ''I don't think so,'' she said. ''You're the only one who has the courage to do anything. They're all waiting on you to get rid of Pendrake.''

''If I did get rid of him, there would just be someone else right behind him, ready to take his place,'' Win said. ''If the people want this town back, they are going to have to take it back. I don't mind getting them started . . . but it is something they have to do for themselves.''

AFTER WIN LEFT, CLAIRE GOT A PENCIL AND PAPER AND began doing some figuring. She worked for about half an hour before she came up with what she believed to be a workable plan. If Harry agreed with her, then she and Harry could go into business together, and they could buy the Desert Flower from Win.

The more she thought about it, the more practical the plan seemed to her, and she actually found herself growing excited about it. She took her figures to Harry, and after some discussion, they decided they would accept Win's proposal.

"Of course, that all depends on whether or not we can live with Pendrake after Win is gone," Harry said.

"I agree," Claire said. "But, like Win said, if we depend on him to get rid of Pendrake, we'll just be the victims of the next son of a bitch who comes along."

"That's true," Harry agreed. He sighed. "I just hope we can convince the other folks in town that we are going to have to take matters into our own hands."

"They'll come around, Harry," Claire said. "You'll see. They'll come around."

For the rest of the day, Claire thought of the possibilities that had been opened up to her by Win's offer. It would be nice to be a property holder, and a woman of some means. She could even buy herself a house and move out of the room she had upstairs. On the downside, however, it would mean that Win would be leaving. And even though she realized that there was really no chance of anything ever developing between the two of them, it would have been nice to keep him around. But she knew she could no sooner do that than she could cage an eagle.

"WHAT DID I TELL YOU?" RANDOL ASKED BEALE, JACKson, and Semmes. "Didn't I tell you the Lord would provide with someone?"

"And you think Coulter is this someone?" Jackson asked.

"Yes. Don't you?"

"I agree that he is someone who is obviously not afraid of Sheriff Pendrake," Jackson said. "But is he someone who is willing to lay it on the line for us?"

"How can you ask that? He made Deputies Wallace and Logan pick up the type after they had scattered it in the street."

"Yes," Jackson said, "after he told Burke to shoot you."

"I have to admit, that gave me cause to worry when he said it, but I've been thinking about it and I know now what he was doing."

"What?"

"He was taking away Burke's one weapon. If you recall, he also told Burke that he expected to be killed as well. I guess he figured if he could put his life on the line, he could put my life on the line too. It was, if I may be honest about it . . . an invigorating experience."

"He is a cool customer, all right," Beale said. "And if you get right down to it, it doesn't matter whether he sticks up for us or not."

"What do you mean by that?" Jackson asked.

"Well . . . he *is* one of us now," Beale said. "After all, he now owns the Desert Flower saloon. So, if he stands up to Pendrake for himself, he is, in effect, standing up for all of us."

"You may have a point, Clem," Randol said. "But what I would like to do is call another meeting of the merchants, this time including Coulter."

"How will we get him to come?" Jackson asked. "I mean, after all, we need him . . . he doesn't need us."

"There is an old saying," Randol replied. "If the mountain won't come to Mohammed, Mohammed will go to the mountain."

"What the hell does *that* mean?" Beale asked.

"We'll hold the meeting in the Desert Flower," Randol said with a satisfied smile.

IT DID NOT TAKE LONG FOR PENDRAKE'S NEW DEPUTY TO make his presence known. When "The Albino," as he was universally called, walked up and down the street of the little town, people shuddered involuntarily at the very sight of him.

"Mama, look at that strange man," a ten-year-old girl said to her mother, when they encountered him on the boardwalk in front of the general store.

The girl's mother put her arms around her daughter and pulled her face into her apron. "Don't look at him, girl," she hissed.

"Why not?" the young girl's muffled voice asked.

"If an unmarried girl looks at someone like that, her milk will turn sour at the birth of her first baby," the mother replied.

Others had their own superstitions about him, saying he had been "touched by Satan," and some even insisted that they could smell a hint of sulphur when they passed by him.

His very appearance was so frightening that people went out of their way to avoid him. Thus it was nearly a week before the first incident.

The Albino was sitting at a table in the back of the Gilded Cage, nursing a drink and playing a game of "Old Sol." It was fitting that he would be playing solitaire, for he was nearly always alone. None of the girls who worked in the saloon would approach him, none of the customers wanted anything to do with him, and even Pendrake's other deputies tended to avoid him. But if being alone bothered The Albino, it didn't show. The second card down was a red nine and there was a black ten on the board. The Albino played the red nine.

The batwing doors swung open and a cowboy came in. He walked up to the bar.

"Let me have a whiskey," he said.

"Sure thing, mister," the bartender answered, filling a glass and pushing it toward him.

The cowboy tossed the drink down, wiped his mouth with the back of his hand, then turned to look out over the saloon.

"My name is Summers. Tully Summers," he said. "That name mean anything to anyone here?"

Summers waited for a long moment to see if anyone would respond. When no one did, he went on: "Me an' my brother owned a spread some miles south of here. His name was Jed. Jed Summers. How about that name? Does it mean anything? I would hope some of you would at least remember his name.''

When there was still no response, he continued. ''Coupla weeks ago, my brother an' some of our hands was comin' back through this town when they run into a little trouble.''

Summers reached for the bottle and poured himself a second drink.

''In any other town they would have been put in jail overnight and allowed to sober up. The next mornin' they would've paid their fines and gone home.'' He was quiet for a moment, and so was the saloon, for there wasn't a person present who didn't know now who and what he was talking about.

''But not in this . . . this hellhole you call a town,'' he said. ''In this place my brother . . . and the others with him, were murdered.''

Still, no one answered.

''I'm told there was a drumhead trial, conducted by someone named Pendrake. I'm told he calls himself a sheriff and a judge. Well, I want to see that man.''

''What do you want to see him for?'' The Albino asked, his words a low hiss. He had not yet risen from the table, and even as he asked the question he didn't look up, as he was seemingly intent on studying the cards in front of him.

''I want Pendrake to look me in the face,'' Tully Summers said. ''I want him to look me right in the eyes. I want him to see the man who is going to kill him.''

''Are you threatening the sheriff?'' The Albino asked. In the week he had been here, The Albino had said very little. That he was engaged in a dialogue now was both fascinating . . . and frightening.

''No,'' Summers replied defiantly. He walked over to stand in front of the table. ''I'm threatening the low-down, sorry son of a bitch who calls himself the sheriff. And that goes for anyone who calls himself a lawman in this town.''

Now The Albino looked up and Summers got a clear look at him. He gasped in surprise as he found himself looking into the expressionless, pink eyes of a face that was as white and cold as death.

"I call myself a lawman," The Albino said quietly.

"Are you . . . are you Pendrake?" Summers asked. Everyone could read exactly what he was thinking. He was wondering if the last thing his brother saw on earth was this apparition.

The Albino shook his head. "I am one of his deputies."

Summers almost breathed a sigh of relief. "I don't want to talk to you," he said. "I want to talk to the sheriff."

"I believe you said that your threat was directed to anyone who calls himself a lawman," The Albino said. "I call myself a lawman. That means your threat was directed at me. Before you see the sheriff, seems like you and me have somethin' to settle."

Summers licked his lips nervously. He had come to Belle Springs on the twin adrenaline-surging emotions of hate and anger. Now that he was here, and face-to-face with the situation, the hate and anger was being replaced by fear. He began to have second thoughts.

"No," he finally said. "We don't have nothin' to settle. I guess I'll just . . . let it go, for now."

Summers turned and started walking away, feeling all eyes on him, fighting against the urge to break into a run.

Someone began to laugh quietly, and near him another joined in, then another, and another still, until within less than half a minute, the entire saloon was roaring with laughter.

"Hey, cowboy, what the hell did you come all this distance for? Just to turn tail and run?" someone taunted.

"Mister, if you try and step through that door, I'll kill you," The Albino said.

Summers froze in his tracks, then he lifted his hands.

"I . . . I don't want no trouble, Deputy," he said. "All I wanted to do is talk to the sheriff about my brother."

"I believe you said that you wanted him to look into the eyes of the man who was going to kill him," The Albino said.

"I was just talkin'," Summers said.

"Turn around."

Summers didn't move.

"I said, turn around."

Summers, still holding his hands up, shook his head. "No," he said. "If I turn around, you'll try and goad me into a fight. Well, I ain't goin' to do it. And I don't believe you want to shoot me in the back in front of all these people."

Suddenly, and shockingly, the room was filled with the roar of a gunshot. There were yells of alarm and surprise as a little spray of blood flew out from the side of Summers's head.

"Son of a bitch! He shot him!" someone shouted.

Summers cried out in pain and slapped his hand to the side of his head. Blood spilled through his fingers, and when he pulled his hand away, everyone saw what had really happened. The lobe of Summers's right ear was a mangled and bloody piece of flesh.

"He shot off his earlobe! My God, have you ever seen shootin' like that?" one of the awed spectators asked aloud.

"Turn around," The Albino said again.

"N-no," Summers stammered. "I ain't goin' to turn around and let you kill me."

The Albino shot again, and this time the tip of the little finger on Summers's left hand was blown away.

With another shout of pain, Summers grabbed his left hand.

"Turn around, or I'll find something else to shoot," The Albino ordered again, his voice no louder this time than it had been on any of the previous times.

Shaking, Summers turned around.

The Albino, who had not yet stood up from the table, put his pistol back in his holster.

"Now, draw," he said.

Summers, in tears now, shook his head. "No," he said. "No, I won't draw on you."

"I'm sitting down," The Albino mocked. "How fast can I be if I am sitting down?"

"I'm not going to draw," Summers said again, "and

there is nothing you can do that will make me.''

Slowly, The Albino took out his pistol and aimed it at Summers. Summers, with tears tracking down his cheeks from tightly closed eyes, just stood there, shaking violently, as he waited for the bullet.

Those in the saloon held their breath, thinking they were about to see an execution. But when the shot came, the ball struck Summers in the kneecap. He went down in agony with both hands, including the bloody left hand, clasped across his shattered knee.

''Get up,'' The Albino said.

''I . . . I can't get up, you son of a bitch!'' Summers said through teeth clenched in pain. ''You shot off my knee-cap!''

''Someone help him up.''

When no one moved, The Albino looked up at two men who were standing closest to Summers's writhing form. He fixed them with his cold, emotionless, pink eyes.

''I said help him up.''

The two men went over to Summers, then, against his protests, pulled him to his feet.

''I . . . I can't stand,'' Summers said.

''Sure you can,'' The Albino replied easily. ''You still got one good knee . . . and I'll let you keep it if you stand there.''

Summers shifted his weight to his good leg. ''What do you want with me?'' he asked. ''For God's sake, mister, let me go.''

''There is no God,'' The Albino said coldly. ''You think if there was a God, He would create someone who looks like me?''

''I . . . I don't know,'' Summers admitted. It was now obvious that he had peed in his pants, but no one said anything. The laughter and taunting that had followed Summers to the door when he attempted to leave earlier was gone now. There wasn't a man in the room who wasn't breathing his own prayer of thanks that it was Summers instead of himself who was receiving all of The Albino's attention.

The Albino put his pistol away. "All right," he finally said. "Go."

"What?"

"I said go," The Albino repeated. He picked up the deck of cards and dealt three out, returning to his game of solitaire.

The two men who had helped Summers to his feet now went over to help him back outside to his horse.

"If I was you, mister, I wouldn't come back here again," one of the men said. "Ever."

"My God!" Summers moaned. "What kind of town is this? What kind of people are you, that you would let madmen like that wear a badge?"

The two men helped Summers onto his horse. One of them handed him his reins, and the other slapped the horse on the rump. The horse started forward at a brisk trot as Summers, fighting the pain and nausea, held on.

The two men watched the horse until it reached the end of the street, then they started to go back inside. One of them stopped, and the other looked around.

"What is it, Fred?"

"I'll tell you the truth, Ernie. You can go back in there if you want to," Fred said. He shook his head. "But I ain't."

"I got to go back in. I still got a drink I paid for, sittin' on the bar," Ernie said.

"Leave it," Fred said. He started down the street toward the Desert Flower.

Ernie hesitated but a moment, then he followed.

12

"IF YOU WANT TO CALL A MERCHANTS' MEETING, YES, I'LL attend," Win told Randol, Beale, and Jackson. "And I'd be glad for you to hold it here."

"Mr. Coulter, the truth is, we'd like more than just your attendance at the meeting," Randol said.

"Like what?"

"Some of us have worked out a plan to put together another city government . . . our own city council, our own mayor . . . independent of the city council and mayor that Pendrake controls."

"Sounds like a reasonable plan," Win agreed.

Randol cleared his throat. "And, uh, we'd like you to be our sheriff."

"In opposition to Pendrake," Jackson said.

"No," Win replied. "I don't think I would be interested in being sheriff, even if you didn't already have one."

Randol shook his head in resignation. "Well, that's it, then. Without your support, our plan doesn't have a chance."

"I didn't say I wouldn't support you," Win said. "I just said I wouldn't be your sheriff."

"Then, I don't understand. What kind of support can we count on?" Beale asked.

"Call your meeting," Win said. "When you get everyone together, I'll speak to them."

Randol smiled broadly. "All right," he said. "We'll meet tonight!"

WHEN WIN WENT INTO DUNNIGAN'S GENERAL STORE THAT afternoon, there were three customers there: a man, a woman, and a boy. The man, who didn't seem to be with the woman, was looking at hats. The woman was over on the other side, unrolling bolts of cloth to examine the fabric. The boy was eyeing a big glass bowl filled with horehound candy.

"Good morning, Mr. Coulter," Dunnigan said when he recognized Win. "I'll be right with you."

"I'm in no hurry," Win replied. He saw the woman looking at him, and he tipped his hat. She made a point of turning away, but before she did, Win saw the look in her eyes, the little lights which glow way in the bottom that said she was curious. If she had the opportunity and no one would ever find out, she would satisfy that curiosity. "Go ahead, take care of the lady," Win said.

"Thank you. Feel free to look around," Dunnigan invited.

Win looked at the boy and saw himself and Joe, when they were youngsters back in Missouri. He could remember when they would go into town with their father. There was always a piece of candy in it for them. Horehound for him, lemon drop for his brother.

Win reached into the bowl and took out a piece of the golden-brown, hard candy, then handed it to the boy.

The boy popped it into his mouth.

"You didn't have to do that," the boy's mother said.

"I know. I did it because I wanted to."

"Well, that was very nice of you. What do you say to the gentleman, Larry?"

"Thanks," the boy said, the word muffled by the candy in his mouth.

"Horehound was always my favorite too," Win said.

"Really? You're not just foolin' me?" the boy asked.

"I'm not just foolin'," Win replied.

"I know who you are," the boy said easily. "You're the one who shot Reeves and Burke, ain't you?"

The smile left Win's face, and he nodded. "I'm the one," he replied.

"Larry, come over here and quit bothering that nice gentleman."

"But don't you know who he is, Mama? He's the one who shot Reeves and Burke. Why, I bet he could kill The Albino."

"Larry!" The woman gasped. "What an awful thing for you to say!"

"But he could do it, Mama, I know he could." Larry looked at Win. "Someday, I'm going to be as good with a gun as you are," he said.

"Son, I hope that someday people won't even feel the need to carry guns," Win replied.

"Mr. Dunnigan, perhaps we had better come back later," the woman suggested, shoving the bolt of cloth back onto the table.

"You needn't hurry off, Mrs. Lawrence. I have two nice bolts of blue cotton in the back that you haven't seen yet," Dunnigan called to her.

"I'll be back," Mrs. Lawrence called over her shoulder, and the bell on the door rang again as she pushed through it, dragging Larry outside with her.

Dunnigan turned toward Win.

"This is for the boy's candy," Win said, handing Dunnigan a penny. "You take care of your customer. I'll look around."

Win busied himself with counting cans of beans until the customer was gone. Then Dunnigan came over to see him.

"Yes, sir, what can I help you with?" he asked.

"You know Harry Conners over at the Desert Flower?"

"Yes, sure, I know him."

"He, Ed Randol, Doc Boyer, Clem Beale, and Arnold Jackson are planning a meeting of all the merchants tonight.

They asked me if I would pass the word around.''

"Are you going to be at the meeting, Mr. Coulter?"
Dunnigan asked.

"Yes, I'm going to be there," Win answered.

"Do you have any idea as to the agenda?"

"Lower taxes."

Dunnigan nodded. "I'm always for lower taxes," he
said. "I'll be there."

Win touched the brim of his hat, then went next door to
the leather goods shop to invite Luther Semmes. In the
meantime, on the opposite side of the street, Joe was making the rounds and carrying the same message. As Win left
the leather goods shop, he saw his brother going into the
feed store. Within half an hour, every businessman and
woman in Belle Springs had been apprised of the meeting
that would be held in the Desert Flower that night.

"SHERIFF, I GOT A FEELIN' SOMETHIN' IS GOIN' ON," WAL-
lace told Pendrake.

"What?"

Wallace shook his head. "I'm not sure, but I've seen
quite a few people goin' into the Desert Flower."

"It's a saloon," Pendrake replied.

"I just seen Helga go in there," Wallace said. "You
know she's not a saloon woman. And Randol and Dunnigan
and Semmes."

"Yeah," Cummins said. "And I seen Jackson from the
hardware store, Deneke from the Feed and Seed, and Beale,
the barber. Hell, even Ling Lee, the Chinaman, is there.
You ain't goin' to get that many merchants together in one
place unless they are havin' a meetin' about somethin' important."

Now Pendrake was interested, and he stroked his chin
for a moment as he thought. "All right, Cummins, go down
there and see what's goin' on," he ordered. "If they are
having a meeting, I want to know about it. And I want to
know what they're talkin' about."

●   ●   ●

THE MEETING WAS BEING HELD IN THE PRIVATE DINING
room of the Desert Flower. Carter, the blacksmith, let fly
a quid of tobacco that made the spittoon ring, while Dunnigan lit up his pipe. When everyone who had been invited
found a seat, Harry got up to talk to them.

"Ladies," he started, with a nod toward Claire and
Helga, "and gentlemen, thank you for coming."

"What's this here meeting all about, Harry?" Carter
asked. "I was told it had somethin' to do with paying lower
taxes."

"Somethin' like that," Harry replied. "To be more specific . . . it's about paying no taxes at all. Leastwise, none
of the sheriff's taxes."

"We can't do that," Semmes said. "If we do, Pendrake
will close us down."

"He won't close down the whole town," Randol said.
"He can't close down the whole town," he added.

"I'm not worried about the whole town, I'm worried
about me."

"Yes," Randol said. "But don't you see? If we all stick
together, then he would have to close down the whole town.
And that, he won't do."

"That's it? That's the reason for this meeting? We're
just going to stop paying taxes?"

"Yes. As I'm sure all of you know, the Desert Flower
has already stopped paying taxes. I've asked Win Coulter,
the owner of the Desert Flower, to share a few words with
us tonight. Mr. Coulter?"

Win stood up and cleared his throat.

"Mr. Randol is right, my brother and I are the new owners of the Desert Flower. And I'm telling you now . . . the
first thing we did was stop paying the sheriff's tax. You
can see what that did for our business."

"That's easy for you to say," one of the businessmen
complained. "The whole town seen how you handled
Reeves and Burke. But none of the rest of us are gunmen."

"No," Win agreed. "But you are citizens of this community. And I want you to stop and think what that means.
This country came through a war not too long ago. My

brother and I were in that war . . . and I imagine some, if not most, of you were. If you were, it doesn't really matter which side you were on. What matters is that you were fighting for what you believed was right. And how anyone who fought in the war could come back here and let a few outlaws take over their town is beyond me.''

"By God, he's right!" Semmes said. "I was at Gettysburg. You got any idea how many men was killed at Gettysburg? How the hell could I go through something like that . . . then come back here and kowtow to a man like Pendrake, and that bunch of coyotes he has around him. Why, his entire force of deputies wouldn't make a pimple on the ass of a good soldier.''

"I was at Gettysburg too," Dunnigan said. He looked at Semmes. "In fact, Semmes, you and I have talked about it before . . . you wore gray, I wore blue. But both of us did our duty.''

"Good for you, Mr. Dunnigan and Mr. Semmes," Win said. "That is just the point I'm trying to make, here. A man like Pendrake has no more power over you than you are willing to give him.''

"All right, Mr. Coulter, we're behind you," Carter said. "Whatever you want to do, we'll support you.''

Win smiled, shook his head, and held out his hands. "No, you are missing the point," he said. "I'm not going to do anything.''

"You ain't goin' to do nothin'?" Carter asked. "Then, I don't understand. What's this all about?''

"Perhaps I can explain," Randol said, speaking again.

"Yeah, please do. I mean, you got us all together, you got our hopes up, now Coulter's tellin' us he ain't interested.''

"That isn't what he is saying at all," Randol replied. "He is very interested. What he is saying is that we are going to have to fight this war for ourselves, just as most of us did once before. It won't work if someone else does it for us. What if we just sat back and let Win Coulter and his brother do everything, fight our battles, and make our decisions? If we did that, we could wind up in the same situation we are now," Randol said.

"Are you saying the Coulters could be as bad as Pendrake and his men?"

"I'm not saying that at all. I'm just saying we should never again turn so much control over to one man . . . as we did with Pendrake."

"I hope you can see that Randol is right," Win said. "None of you really know my brother or me. You shouldn't be that anxious to let us handle everything just because it's easy for you. Anything worth having is worth fighting for, and you don't deserve anything if you don't have the gumption to hang on to it."

"All right, so what do we do now?"

"Doc?" Randol said. "I believe you have a plan you want to share with us?"

Doc Boyer stood up and cleared his throat. "I hereby make the motion that this body be declared to be an acting city council, with all powers to create and enforce city laws and ordinances."

"What about the current city council?" someone asked.

"What city council?" Harry replied with a smirk. "That frightened bunch of old men are the ones who got us into this mess in the first place."

"But what you are suggesting here is a revolution."

Harry thought about it for a moment, then he chuckled. "I suppose we are making a revolution. But if we are, so what? It was good enough for our forefathers, it is good enough for us."

"So what do we do now?"

"Now," Doc said, "we have to have someone second my motion. Do we have any seconds?"

"I second that motion," Claire said. Until now, she had remained silent.

"You can't second the motion, Claire," Harry said. "You're a woman, and women don't have the vote."

"So what does that mean?" Claire shot back. "When is the last time *anyone* in this town voted?"

"Claire has a point," Randol said with a chuckle.

"We're in this together, so I figure the women have as much right to have a say in this as the men."

Doc grinned at Claire. "All right, Claire, you seconded it. Now, the motion has been made and seconded, that we act as a town council. All in favor say aye."

"Aye," several voices said as one.

"It is unanimous."

"Mr. Randol, I wonder if you would act as our mayor?" Doc proposed. His proposal was seconded, so that a moment later Ed Randol, publisher of the Belle Springs newspaper, became the de facto mayor of Belle Springs.

"I thank you for your vote of confidence," Randol said. "Now, as our first act, I recommend that we repeal the sheriff's tax. And remember, this must be unanimous. If anyone goes back on this one . . . you will put all the rest of us in danger."

There was a spirited discussion over that proposal, but before the council finished its business that evening, the act passed. Every businessman in Belle Springs left the meeting with the resolve to pay no more taxes to the sheriff.

FOR THE ENTIRE MEETING, DEPUTY CUMMINS HAD BEEN sitting at a table in the main room of the Desert Flower. Although he was actually outside the meeting room, he was close enough to the open door to hear most, if not all, of what went on. He heard them make the declaration that they would refuse to pay the sheriff's taxes from now on, and that was the news he took to Pendrake.

"Damn!" Wallace said. "What are we going to do about that? I mean, if all the businesses stop paying the taxes, where are we going to get our money?"

"They aren't going to stop paying their taxes," Pendrake said.

"They sounded pretty set to me, Sheriff," Cummins said. "It's the Coulter brothers who have them all fired up. Especially Win Coulter."

Pendrake smiled. "Well, then," he said, "I suppose we'll just have to get rid of Win Coulter, won't we? Mr. Black?"

The Albino had been sitting quietly in the corner of the office, seemingly paying no attention to their discussion. Now he looked up in a silent response to Pendrake's summons.

"Take care of Mr. Coulter for us," Pendrake ordered.

The Albino nodded, then stood up and left the office.

"I don't care if he is on our side," Wallace said after The Albino was gone. "That son of a bitch gives me the creeps."

13

WIN WAS STANDING AT THE BAR, TALKING WITH HARRY and Claire. Joe was upstairs with Lily. Most of the others who had attended the business meeting were, by now, back at their own place of business or in their homes. Doc was sitting in a poker game at the rear of the saloon.

This was the setting when The Albino pushed his way in through the double batwing doors. He stood there for a moment, his pink eyes moving slowly around the room until they located Win.

"Win Coulter!" The Albino said. His raised voice contained enough of a challenging edge to arrest everyone's attention.

Win looked around. "You talking to me, maggot?"

These were obviously fighting words, and the customers in the saloon began scurrying, pushing tables aside and knocking over chairs in their haste to get out of the way.

"I'm here to collect the tax."

"What tax?"

"The sheriff's tax," The Albino said.

"You go back and tell the sheriff we've repealed that tax," Win said. He turned back to the bar.

"The sheriff ain't goin' to like that."

"If the sheriff doesn't like our laws, tell him to go find another town," Win said.

The Albino shook his head. "It doesn't work that way, Coulter. You're going to set a good example by paying the tax, now, in front of all these people."

"And if I don't?"

"Then I'm going to have to kill you," The Albino said easily. "Draw."

Win smiled. "Suppose we go outside?" he said. "There's less chance of someone else getting hurt."

For just a moment a flicker of doubt flashed in The Albino's otherwise unreadable eyes. He had seen every reaction imaginable in the faces of his victims when he confronted them. He had never before seen one smile. Win's smile unnerved him.

Win turned to say something to Harry. As he did so, he saw something in the mirror behind the bar. The Albino was going for his gun.

Win was fast, and had he been facing The Albino in a fair draw, he might have beaten him. But The Albino was also fast, incredibly fast, and by the time Win turned, with his gun in his hand, The Albino was already firing. Win tried to pull the trigger to return fire, but when The Albino's bullet hit him, the entire upper half of his body went instantly numb. He sent the message to his trigger finger to fire, but his trigger finger was unable to react.

The impact of the bullet slammed Win back against the edge of the bar. He hit it, then slid down to the floor in a sitting position. Harry hurried around from the bar toward him, and dimly Win heard someone shouting his name. Sounds seemed to come to him from far down in a cave and, though he knew they were talking about him, it was almost as if they were in another room, talking about someone else, and he was a distant and disinterested listener.

Doc came quickly to Win's side. Win saw him coming toward him, then his vision dimmed, and finally went black.

"How is he, Doc?" Claire asked, her voice on the edge of panic. "How is he?"

Doc put his hand on Win's neck and held it there for a moment, then he sighed and shook his head slowly.

"I'm sorry, Claire," he said. "Win is dead."

The Albino stepped around behind the bar and took a bottle of whiskey from the shelf. He poured himself a drink.

"You folks didn't really need a doctor to tell you that," he hissed. "I could've told you he was dead from the moment I pulled the trigger."

"You . . . you maggot-faced bastard!" Claire screamed, and she started toward him.

The Albino pulled his pistol and fired into the ceiling. The sudden, unexpected thunderclap of another gunshot stopped Claire's charge, and The Albino lowered his pistol and pointed it at her.

"You'd better stop right there, lady," he said. "If you think I won't shoot you just because you're a woman, then you got another think comin'. Killin' is killin'. It's what I do and I'm pretty damned good at my work."

"Back away from him, Claire, please," Harry said.

"You'd better listen to the barkeep, lady," The Albino warned.

Claire turned away from him and put her hands to her eyes. She was sobbing out loud.

"Couple of you fellas take that door down," Doc ordered, pointing to the door that opened into the kitchen. "Let's put Win on it and get him down to Luscomb's funeral parlor. Claire, you want to come along with us?"

"Oh, Doc, I don't know," Claire said between sobs. "I don't know if I can take it."

The door was taken down and Win was picked up and put carefully onto it.

"Where's Joe?" Doc said, looking around.

"He was upstairs, last I knew," Harry said.

"Get word to him. Tell him what happened."

"I will," Harry said, looking up. "It's funny he didn't come down when he heard the gunshot."

"All right, men, let's get this body down to the funeral parlor." At Doc's direction, the sad little party left the saloon. "Claire, I think you had better come."

"Doc, I . . ."

"I need you to come, Claire. Can't you do this much for him?" Doc challenged.

"I . . . yes, of course," Claire said. "I'll come with you."

Those who had moved out of the way during the shooting now began to return, and tables and chairs were repositioned as the saloon patrons took their seats and resumed their activity. Conversation started again, but it was hushed and whispered.

JOE HAD REACHED THE TOP OF THE STAIRS JUST AS THE doctor pronounced his brother dead. Seeing The Albino standing behind the bar with a gun in his hand made it fairly easy to figure out what happened. It was very hard for Joe to do nothing at that precise moment, because all instinct told him to charge his brother's murderer and attack him with his bare hands. But The Albino was armed and, at the moment, Joe was not. To confront The Albino now would have been a very foolish thing to do.

Prudently, Joe turned and went back up the stairs, then down to the end of the hallway, where he stepped through the window, climbed out onto the mansard roof, then dropped down to the ground. Once on the ground, he ran quickly down the alley until he reached the hardware store. Entering through the back door, he saw Jackson standing behind the counter. Jackson looked up, smiling.

"Hello, Joe," he said. "I was just about to close for the day. What are you doing coming in through the back door?"

"It was quicker," Joe replied without explanation. He pointed to the shotgun rack. "Would you let me borrow that Greener, ten-gauge, double-barrel for a few minutes?" he asked.

"Borrow it?" Jackson replied, curious as to the strange request. "Well, sure, I suppose so." As Jackson took the gun from the rack, Joe opened a box of shells and removed two.

"Thanks," Joe said, taking the gun and going back out

through the alley door. Jackson watched him leave, curious as to what was going on.

When Joe looked in through the back door at the Desert Flower, he saw that the place was still buzzing over what had just happened. He saw also that his brother's body and The Albino were gone. Quietly and without being seen, he stepped back out into the alley.

Joe moved along the outside wall of the Desert Flower from the back to the front. When he reached Main Street he looked down to the south end of the street where he saw The Albino just going into the Gilded Cage. Shoving the two shells into the breech of the shotgun, he snapped it shut, then purposefully strode down the middle of Main Street toward the Gilded Cage.

Joe thought about what had just happened. He had known for a long time that this moment might come. He and Win had faced death many times, starting with when they had ridden for Quantrill. They had talked about it, and had prepared each other for it.

"When it happens . . ." Win had said during one of their conversations.

"You mean, if it happens, don't you?" Joe replied.

Win had put his hand on Joe's shoulder then. "All right, Little Brother, if you want to think of it that way," he said easily. "Though in our business, it is much better to think of it as when, rather than if. But if . . . and . . . when it happens, the best thing to do would be for whichever one of us is left to just get on with his life."

At the time, Joe agreed with his brother, and he was perfectly willing to do that now. The only thing was, he knew he would not be able to get on with his life until he had settled accounts with The Albino.

About one minute later, Joe stepped through the front door of the Gilded Cage. From the back of the room, the piano was grinding away in an off-key rendition of "Buffalo Gals." The room was noisy with a dozen or more animated conversations. Joe looked around the room and located The Albino sitting alone at a table in the back. Cards from The Albino's incessant game of solitaire were spread out on the table before him. Joe realized that he must've left the game, then come back to it. That made him even angrier, as if killing his brother had been so inconsequential to him that The Albino didn't even bother to quit his game . . . he just left the cards where they were.

Although many others in Joe's current frame of mind would have called out, cursing in anger and challenge the moment they stepped through the door, Joe did none of that. Nor did he do anything else to call attention to himself. Amazingly, his arrival was practically unnoticed by any of the saloon's patrons. Almost as if he were invisible, Joe walked back to The Albino's table. Not until then did The Albino look up.

"Ah," The Albino said. There was not the slightest hint of surprise on his face. "I didn't think I'd have to come looking for you. I was pretty sure you would come to me . . . to avenge your brother. And so here you are, come to test yourself against me. Do you really think you can beat me?"

In a sudden, totally unexpected, and incredibly fast move, Joe whipped the butt of the shotgun around to smash in The Albino's face. The Albino's nose practically exploded under the blow, and the blood that erupted so quickly made a bright, crimson smear against his otherwise chalky-white face. With blood and teeth flying, The Albino was knocked from his chair. He landed flat on his back, and, so powerful was the blow, that he slid for a few feet across the floor.

The blow had also rattled his senses, so that The Albino was hanging on to the narrow line between consciousness and unconsciousness. Joe didn't hit him again. He wanted him conscious. He wanted him to know what was happening to him.

The Albino looked up at Joe in total confusion, his pink eyes swimming as he tried to figure out how he'd wound up lying on the floor, and when he had lost the advantage.

"You want me to test myself against you?" Joe said coldly. "Don't you understand yet, you worthless piece of dog shit? I'm not here for any fight. I'm here to kill you."

Without another word, Joe raised the shotgun to his shoulder and pulled one of the two triggers. At the last minute, The Albino *did* understand, and his pink eyes grew red in terror just before his face was blown away by the deafening blast of the shotgun. When the smoke cleared away, even the most hardened were sickened by the bloody mess that lay on the floor.

Joe turned angrily to face the others in the saloon. A tiny wisp of smoke was still curling up from the end of the barrel he had just discharged.

"I've got one load left," he said. "If anyone wants a taste of it, try me."

He leveled the gun, then began swinging it from side to side. The customers in the saloon moved quickly to get out of his way, and no one made any attempt to keep him from leaving.

Joe went directly to the stable. With Win dead, there was no need for him to stay any longer. And with so many witnesses to what had just happened in the saloon, he figured the best thing for him to do would be to leave town. In no longer than it took for him to saddle his horse, Joe was on his way, leaving the shotgun behind to be returned to Jackson. Only now did he allow himself to grieve for his brother.

14

WHAT JOE DID NOT REALIZE WAS THAT HIS GRIEF WAS premature. Win wasn't dead, and Doc Boyer knew that even when he made the pronouncement. As he explained to Claire when he was able to get her alone, "I was afraid that if The Albino knew he hadn't killed him, he might finish the job."

"Thank God he isn't dead!" Claire said.

"Not yet, anyway."

"Not yet? How bad is he?"

"Shh!" Doc cautioned. He pointed to the men ahead, who were carrying Win. "Don't let them hear us," he cautioned. Then he answered Claire's question. "The bullet passed all the way through, and I don't think it hit any of the vitals. If it had, he would probably already be dead. The next couple of days will tell the story. If the wound doesn't begin to fester, he should pull through all right."

"What if one of the deputies finds out—"

"They aren't going to find out," Doc said. "No one knows but you. And if you want to keep him safe . . . and me alive as well for what I did tonight, then you mustn't tell a soul."

"But, Doc, I have to tell Joe," Claire said. "Joe's his brother. He has a right to know."

"All right, I agree. You can tell Joe, but no one else."

Claire looked at Win's still form, stretched out on the door.

"Are you sure he is still alive? He doesn't look it. I mean, look at him. He is so still."

"Did you see the handkerchief I was holding in my hand when I examined him?"

"Yes."

"It was soaked with chloroform. I gave him a pretty good dose, enough to keep him knocked out for at least half an hour. I thought it would be imprudent for him to suddenly wake up and make me look like a fool."

"What about Luscomb?" Claire asked.

"What about him?"

"He's the undertaker. He'll know, won't he? I mean, as soon as he examines the body?"

"Yes. He'll know. But don't worry about him. He owes me several favors. It's about time he paid them back."

Doc and Claire were following along behind the men carrying Win's prostrate form, laid out on a door. And they were talking so quietly that although the four volunteers were just in front of them, they couldn't hear what was being said.

By the time they got there, word had already reached Luscomb, and he was standing outside the door to the funeral parlor.

"My, what a tragedy," Luscomb said. He stepped back from the door and held his hand out in invitation. "Please, take him inside and put him on the embalming table."

The volunteers carried Win inside, then lifted him off the door and laid him on a porcelain table that was surrounded by tubes and tanks.

"That will be all, men, thank you," Doc said.

"Mind if I stay and watch?" one of the men asked.

"Stay if you wish," Luscomb said.

"No," Doc interjected. "I want everyone out."

"Doc, I don't mind if anyone watches, it doesn't bother me."

"I want everyone out," Doc said again.

"All right, Doc, whatever you say," the man who had asked to stay replied. "I just ain't never seen no one embalmed, is all."

"I'm going to perform an autopsy," Doc said more gently. "It's the final invasion of privacy, and I don't like anyone around."

"Autopsy?" Luscomb said. "Hell, Doc, what you need an autopsy for? I can tell you how he died. He was shot."

"There are other reasons for performing autopsies than determining the cause of death," Doc said. "You men, go back to the saloon. Drink all you want. Tell Harry the drinks are on me."

The four men smiled broadly. "Thanks, Doc," they said, hurrying out of the door.

Doc turned to Claire then. "Claire, you might want to find Joe."

"All right," Claire said.

"When you find him, bring him here."

Doc walked back to the door with Claire, shutting it behind her and locking it after she left.

"Hey, Doc!" Luscomb called, the tone of his voice elevated in excitement. He was beginning to examine the body. "Hey, Doc, you'd better get over here. You need to see this!"

"Quiet!" Doc said.

"But, Doc, he—"

Doc turned around and held his hand out. "Please, Mr. Luscomb, I know what you are going to say . . . so don't say it."

"You want to tell me what's going on?" Luscomb asked, when Doc returned to the table and opened one of Win's eyes to examine the pupil.

Doc explained what he had done, and why.

"Well, how do you plan to keep such a thing a secret?" he asked.

"By burying him."

"Burying him?"

"Or, at least, by burying a weighted coffin," Doc said.

"You expect me to bury an empty coffin? Listen, those things are expensive, and—"

"Don't worry about your coffin," Doc said. "You'll be paid for it."

Their conversation was interrupted by a loud, impatient knock. Doc went over to the door.

"Doc, it's me, Claire! Let me in!"

Doc opened the door and Claire stepped inside. She was pale-looking, and the expression on her face was one of shock and horror.

"What is it, Claire? What's wrong?"

"It's Joe."

"What about him? Where is he?"

"He's gone. Doc, he thought Win was dead, so he took a shotgun over to the Gilded Cage and killed The Albino."

Doc sighed. "Damn," he said. "I wish I had been able to get word to him before this happened." He snorted what could have been a chuckle. "On the other hand, if he killed The Albino . . . all I can say is, good riddance."

"Doc," Luscomb called from the embalming table.

"Yes?"

"He's comin' around."

There was another loud knock on the door. "Luscomb! Luscomb, you in there?"

While Doc was tending to the awakening Win, Luscomb opened the door to see who was calling him.

"They need you over to the Gilded Cage, Luscomb," the man at the door said. "Joe Coulter just about blew The Albino's head off."

"So I just heard," Luscomb said. "All right, I'll be right there." He looked over his shoulder at Doc and Win, then added, "The one I got in here sure isn't going anywhere."

The man outside laughed. "Ain't goin' anywhere. That's a good one," he said.

MORBID CURIOSITY HAD DRAWN SO MANY PEOPLE TO THE Gilded Cage that the crowd spilled through the front doors and out onto the plank sidewalk. Luscomb had to literally push his way through.

"Let me through, please, let me through," he said as he worked his way inside.

"Hey, it's the undertaker. Let him through. Let him through."

When Luscomb reached the scene he saw several people crowded around one spot, looking toward the floor. At first, Luscomb could see only an overturned chair and the bottom of The Albino's boots.

Pendrake was leaning against the bar, holding a beer. "Get him out of here," he growled, nodding toward The Albino's sprawled body. Someone had draped a cloth across The Albino's head and shoulders. As he lay on the ground his feet were turned out and his hands were by his side, palms up. The pistol was still in his gun belt, for he had not made the slightest move toward it. He had been so smugly confident of his speed and skill with a gun that he had not had the remotest idea that he could be in any danger from a man like Joe Coulter.

The Albino's problem was that he thought of his pistol as a work of art, a thing of beauty, and the use of the gun, the ability to draw and fire quickly, he regarded as chore-ography. The Albino had studied other skilled gunmen. He knew how many men each had killed, he knew the glory they had attained, and he could measure their speed in in-crements as precise as the blink of an eye.

He knew, also, that there weren't more than two or three men in the entire country who would stand a chance against him. One of those men was Win Coulter, and he had made use of that knowledge, choosing the time to put Coulter down, using the "edge" of starting his draw when Coul-ter's back was to him. He knew, also, that of the two Coulter brothers, Win was, by far, the more skilled gunman.

It was what The Albino *didn't* know about Joe that got him killed. To Joe a gun was nothing but a tool, like a shovel, or a plow. Joe didn't study tools, he used them. He went to the saloon with only one purpose in mind, and that was to kill The Albino. And, in the fulfillment of that purpose, he made excellent use of the tool he was holding in his hand, a double-barreled, ten-gauge, Greener shotgun.

The result was the disfigured corpse Luscomb was now examining.

Luscomb pulled the cloth back and looked at what used to be The Albino's face. It looked like a piece of liver.

"There's no way I can ever fix his face for viewing," Luscomb said.

"Hell, no one could stand to look at the ugly son of a bitch while he was alive," Pendrake growled. "Who would want to look at him dead? Forget about trying to do anything to his face."

"You will be paying for his funeral?" Luscomb asked. "How much will it cost?"

"Well, there's the embalming, and the clothes, and the coffin. I'm sure you'll want the best coffin . . . and, of course, you'll want to bury him in a manner befitting one of your deputies, so I would say—"

"Forget the embalming," Pendrake said with an impatient wave of his hand. "And the coffin. Just wrap the bastard in a piece of tarpaulin and put him in the ground. And do it tonight," he added. "There's no sense in keeping the ugly son of a bitch around any longer than we have to."

IN THE NEXT TWENTY-FOUR HOURS AN INTERESTING DI-chotomy took place in Belle Springs.

In the manner of George Black, The Albino, there was a corpse without a funeral.

In the manner of Win Coulter, there was a funeral without a corpse.

On the day of Win's funeral, the Desert Flower was closed. So were all the other businesses up and down Main Street. The only exception was the Gilded Cage. It was open, but it too was practically empty, with only four or five customers who weren't wearing a deputy's badge.

"Where the hell is ever'body?" Pendrake asked as he stepped up to the bar. The bartender moved down to him, then selected a bottle from under the bar. Unlike the bottles on the shelves behind the bar, this one had a label, indicating it was a better stock than that normally served to Gilded Cage customers.

"Why, Sheriff, they are all at Win Coulter's funeral," the bartender said. "Haven't you noticed? The whole town is closed up . . . stores, shops, even the bank."

At that moment the church bell began to peal.

"What are they ringin' the bell for?" Pendrake asked.

"They got to," the bartender replied.

"What do you mean, they got to?"

"Ain't you never heard? You got to ring the bell the same number of times as the number of years the dead person lived. Otherwise, his soul is lost in Limbo."

"Lost in Limbo? What does that mean?"

"It means the soul don't go to Heaven or Hell. It just wanders around."

"You mean like a ghost?" Wallace asked. He and Cummins had been listening to the conversation.

"Yeah, sort of like that, I suppose," the bartender answered.

"Oooooooohhh. I'm the ghost of Win Coulter!" Cummins moaned, and the others laughed.

"Shut up!" Pendrake ordered. He turned away from the bar and pointed at his deputies, and the few others who were still in the saloon. "All of you, just shut the hell up!"

"Hey, come on, Sheriff," Wallace said. "We didn't mean nothin' by it. We was just funnin' a little, that's all."

"Yeah, well any more funnin' like that and I'll turn one of you into a real ghost, if you get my meanin'," Pendrake said menacingly.

"We get your meanin'," Cummins said.

Pendrake walked to the door of the saloon and looked down the north end of the street at the church. The front doors of the church had been thrown open, and at that moment, six men were coming through the door, carrying a coffin. Gingerly, they came down the steps, then slid the coffin into the back of the hearse. Others began pouring out of the church then, and, within a few moments, a procession was formed. With the hearse leading the way, the funeral cortege started south on Main Street. In just a moment or two, they would be passing in front of the Gilded Cage, then they would turn west on Second Street, on their way to the cemetery. Some of the mourners rode in carriages or wagons, some rode horses, but nearly as many walked.

"Get over here," Pendrake said gruffly. "All of you. Get over here and show some respect for the dead." Pendrake took off his hat.

"Sheriff, you can't be serious. You ain't never showed respect for any dead before. Besides which, you're the one who told The Albino to kill him."

"I'm very serious," Pendrake said coldly.

With a shrug of his shoulders, Wallace looked at Cummins, then the others who were in the saloon. To a man, they rose and walked over to the front door. Pendrake moved out onto the porch and indicated that they should do the same. Then, as the funeral cortege passed by, Pendrake, his deputies, and the few patrons of Pendrake's saloon stood by silently, with their heads bared.

Claire, dressed in black, and wearing a long, black veil, rode in the first buggy behind the hearse. The buggy was being driven by Harry Conners. When Claire saw Pendrake and the others makng a gesture of respect she looked pointedly away from them.

AFTER THE FUNERAL, HARRY STOPPED THE BUGGY IN front of the Desert Flower, then helped Claire down.

"How long do you think we should stay shut?" Harry asked.

"I'd say at least three days," Claire replied. "Don't you think?"

"Yes," Harry said. "Win Coulter was a good man. A damn good man. We won't see his kind around again, for a while."

In keeping her promise to Doc Boyer, Claire had not shared with Harry the fact that Win was still alive. She reached out to lay her fingers on his hand.

"Maybe we will, Harry," she said. "Sooner than you think."

Once inside the saloon, Claire walked through the quiet

bar area. It was lighted by splashes of sunlight that managed to find its way in through the cracks and gaps of the closed window shutters. Claire pulled the hat pin from her stiffened hat and took it and the veil off, wadding the little bits of cloth and stiffener in her hands as she climbed the stairs to the top floor. When she reached the top of the stairs she looked down toward the closed doors of what had been Win's and Joe's rooms, sighed, then moved quickly toward her own room.

"How did the funeral go?" Doc Boyer asked just as Claire was letting herself in.

"It went fine."

"Anybody say anything about my not being there?"

"Not that I overheard," Claire said. "Maybe nobody even noticed. The funeral was very well attended. Nearly everyone in town was there."

"Well, of course it would be," Doc said. "Most of the people in this town had put their hopes in Win being able to save them. Were you surprised that it was so well attended?"

"No. I mean, I guess I knew there would be a crowd. It's just that, well, Doc, I don't know. I feel like we're being dishonest with everyone in the town."

"Maybe we are," Doc agreed. "But we can't afford to let anyone know what's going on. At least, not yet. And when the people find out what we did, and why we did it, they'll forgive us. Believe me, Claire, they will forgive us."

"I suppose so. How is the patient doing?"

"He's sleeping. You want to look in on him?"

"Yes," Claire said. She walked into her room and looked inside. There, on the bed, his chest swathed in bandages and his eyes closed in troubled sleep, lay Win Coulter. "Is he going to make it?" she asked.

"It's looking better. It's been two days now, and still no signs of wound mortification. And every day he stays alive is one day of getting stronger."

"He's going to make it," Claire said. "I know he is."

"Claire, I'm going to have to depend on you to take care of all the nursing," Doc Boyer said. "You're going to have

to keep his bandages changed, keep him clean and warm.
It's going to take an awful lot of hard work.''

"Hard work I can provide," Claire said. "I don't know
about my nursing skills, though.''

Doc Boyer reached out and patted Claire on the hand.
"I have faith in you, Claire," he said. "As far as I'm concerned, Win wouldn't have any better chance if he was in
the finest hospital in the world. Now, I've got to get out
and be seen around town. I'll drop back in to check on him
tomorrow.''

"All right, Doc," Claire said. "And thanks for everything.''

After Doc Boyer left, Claire pulled up a rocking chair
and sat next to Win's bed. She rocked back and forth
slowly, all the while looking into Win's face. It was a nice
face. There might have been faces more handsome, but
none more pleasing to her eyes.

Win's eyes were closed now, but she wished they were
open. His eyes were the most fascinating feature about his
face. They were deep and dark blue, and when she looked
into them long enough and hard enough, she would sometimes feel herself spinning away into dizziness, like trying
to contemplate eternity.

"Win," she said softly. "Win, I know you can't hear
me now, but I want to tell you that I'm not going to let
you die. Do you hear me? I am not going to let you die!''

Claire raised up in her chair a little to see if her words
had had any effect on Win. It didn't appear that they had.

"I don't know where Joe is right now. He killed the
bastard who shot you, then he left town. But I can't get
over the feeling that we'll hear from him again, and when
we do, I'll let him know the truth. And when he learns that
you aren't dead, he'll be as happy as I was. And it was
almost worth the despair to have that joy.''

15

"No!" Win suddenly shouted. At the cry, he sat up in bed and swung his legs over the edge so quickly that Claire, who had been dozing in the rocking chair, was startled awake. "I've got to warn Quantrill!" Win shouted. He tried to stand up.

"Win! Win, what are you doing? You'll open your wound. You'll start bleeding again!"

"Excuse me, ma'am," Win said. He looked toward the door. "Joe! Joe, get in here! Where is Joe? We've got to get word to Quantrill."

"Win, Win, it's me, Claire! Don't you recognize me?"

Win looked at Claire with eyes that were burning with intensity. "Claire! What are you doing here?" he asked. "You've got to get out of here! The battle is going to begin at any moment! The Yankees are massing on the other side of the trees!"

"Win, listen to me!" Claire said. "That war is over. Do you hear me? That war is over. You are safe now. You are here, in my bedroom."

"Your bedroom?" Win asked, sitting back down on the edge of the bed. He put his hand over his wound and it

came away bloody. Win looked around in confusion. "I
am in your bedroom," he said. "What am I doing in
here?"

"You've been shot," Claire said.

Win looked down at his chest. "Yes," he said dryly.
"Well, I may not know what the hell is going on, but I can
tell that I have been shot. It hurts like hell."

"Lie back down," Claire ordered. "I need to change the
dressing now."

"All right," Win said, obeying her order without question.

Claire poured some water into a basin and brought it over
to put on the little table beside the bed. Gingerly, she began
removing his old bandage, then started bathing the wound.

"I remember now," Win said. "It was The Albino,
wasn't it?"

"Yes."

Win looked around the room. "What am I doing in here?
Why aren't I down at the doc's office?"

"Doc thought it would be best to keep you out of sight,"
Claire said.

"Out of sight?"

"He thought it would be safer."

"Look here! Are you telling me I am *hiding* from that
maggot bastard?" Win tried to stand up.

"No," Claire said. "You don't have to hide from him.
He's dead."

"Dead? Did I kill him?"

"No. Joe did."

"Joe? But I don't understand. As fast as The Albino is,
how could Joe . . ."

"From what I hear," Claire said as she continued to
work, "your brother just walked into the Gilded Cage with
a shotgun and blew The Albino's head off without so much
as a fair thee well."

Win laughed, then grabbed himself in the chest. "That
hurts," he said. "Yeah, that's the way Joe would do it, all
right. He is pretty methodical about things. Where is he
now?"

"Nobody knows. As soon as he killed The Albino, he left town."

"Well, he'll get in touch."

Claire looked at Win with a pained expression on her face.

"What is it?" Win asked. "What's wrong?"

"Win, Joe thinks you are dead."

"He thinks I'm dead?"

"Doc was there when you were shot. He examined you, then pronounced you dead. That was to keep The Albino from finishing you off. Then Doc thought it might be safer to let everyone think that."

"Didn't anyone think Joe might have a right to know?"

"I went to tell him," Claire said. "But before I could find him, he had already killed The Albino and left."

"Damn," Win said.

"I'm sorry."

Win lifted his hand and put it on Claire's arm. "No," he said. "It isn't your fault. You and Doc did what you thought was right . . . and under the circumstances, who is to argue with you? Don't worry, I'll find Joe."

IT WAS MID-AFTERNOON AND THE SUN WAS A BRILLIANT orb halfway down its western transit when Joe saw the town of McKee rising into view on the plains before him. Sunlight shimmered off the shingled roofs and clapboard sidings of the dozen or so buildings of the town. The tallest structure of the town was the water tower, down by the depot.

McKee was a busy town. Board sidewalks clattered with the footsteps of men and women who were tending to their daily business, a couple of full freight wagons lumbered down the single dirt street, while, over at the leather company, rendering pots simmered and stunk as hides were being tanned.

Joe rode through the town till he reached the first saloon. There, he tied his horse off out front, then went in to have a drink. Two men, close by, were involved in conversation.

When he heard Belle Springs mentioned, he began paying attention.

"It was over to Belle Springs that it happened," one of the two men said. "The way I heard it, Tully Summers went over there to find out what happened to his brother an' his hands, and he got near shot to pieces by one of the deputies they got over there."

"Belle Springs? I was over to Belle Springs couple years ago. I thought that was a pretty nice town."

"It did, use to be. Till Harley Pendrake come along. He's sheriff over there now, and he's got hisself a bunch of mean deputies. From what I hear, Belle Springs ain't a fit place to live . . . ain't even a place a fella would want to visit anymore."

"Why don't they elect 'em a new sheriff?"

"Elect? Hell, they didn't elect Pendrake. He buffaloed the town council into appointin' him. And from what I hear, the town council is too scared to even meet anymore, so there's no way to get rid of him."

"That's a shame. There's some pretty good folks over there. Somebody ought to do somethin'."

"Like what?"

"I don't know. Write a letter or somethin'."

The first man snorted. "Write a letter. Arnie, you talk like a man with a paper asshole. What the hell good is writin' a letter goin' to do?"

"I don't know," the one called Arnie replied. "But seems to me like somebody ought to do somethin'."

"Want another?" the bartender asked, moving down the bar to stand in front of Joe, just as Joe was finishing his beer.

"Uh, no, thanks," Joe said. "One was enough."

The conversation made Joe realize that he should've stayed in Belle Springs to finish what he and his brother had started. He hadn't been thinking clearly when he left. He had killed The Albino because the son of a bitch needed killing . . . then he left town because that seemed to be the natural thing to do.

It might have been the natural thing, he decided, but not

the best thing. The best thing would be to go back and help the town get rid of Pendrake. And not just because he was a do-gooder. After all, he had an economic interest to protect. He and Win . . . Joe paused. No, not he and Win . . . Win was gone and Joe was going to have to get used to thinking that way. He—Joe—owned a saloon in Belle Springs, and he would be damned if he'd let Pendrake take it away from him.

When Joe stepped into the depot, the stationmaster and the telegrapher were engaged in an intense conversation about Lillie Langtry. The question seemed to be whether or not she was more beautiful than Cleopatra. The train master was sure that she was.

"Don't get me wrong," the telegrapher said. "I ain't sayin' she ain't prettier than Cleopatra. I'm just sayin' that there ain't no one alive who ever seen Cleopatra, so there's no way of knowin'."

"Didn't anyone ever draw a picture of Cleopatra?" the stationmaster wanted to know.

"I don't know. I don't think so."

"Then how the hell do we know if she was even pretty at all, let alone prettier than Lillie Langtry? No, sir, I'm tellin' you that Lillie Langtry is the prettiest woman what ever lived, and I'm stickin' by that claim," the stationmaster said. He turned his attention to Joe. "What can I do for you, mister?"

"What time's the next train for Belle Springs?"

"Tomorrow mornin', at six o'clock."

"Nothing before then? Not even a freight?"

"Well, there's a freight leavin' at nine tonight. It'll get into Belle Springs at midnight. It won't be fittin' to ride on, though. No passenger cars attached."

"I'll ride in a stock car with my horse."

"You'll have to pay for your horse and yourself."

"That's all right," Joe said. "I want to get there tonight."

JOE WAS ASLEEP IN THE HAY WHEN THE TRAIN STOPPED AT the Belle Springs station at a little after midnight. He thanked the freight handler for putting up the ramp that allowed him to lead his horse off the car, then he took the horse back to the livery where he had been keeping him.

Most of the town was quiet, though there was still some activity down at the Gilded Cage. The Desert Flower, however, was as dark as the general store, the apothecary, the bank, and all the other businesses in town.

Joe moved through the shadows until he reached the Desert Flower. The doors were locked, but he still had a key to the back door, and he used the key to let himself in. Once inside, he went upstairs and knocked lightly on the door to Lily's room.

The door opened, and Lily peeked through the crack.

"Joe!" she said.

"Shh!" Joe cautioned.

Lily opened the door and Joe stepped inside.

"What are—"

"We'll talk later," Joe said. He put his hand on her chin, then lifted her head up so he could kiss her. He didn't know if, under the circumstances, she would welcome him, but the urgency of her response and the eagerness of her tongue put his doubts to rest.

"Wait," she said breathlessly after their first kiss. "Let me light a candle."

Joe waited until a tiny pillar of flame stood atop a white taper, illuminating the room in a soft, golden glow. He watched as Lily slipped out of the chemise she had been sleeping in, so that she stood by the bed, totally naked. Then, hurriedly, he slipped out of his own clothes.

Lily moved to him, and Joe put his hand on her inner thigh, then moved it up. He slid his finger down through the lips of her sex, feeling the slickness of her desire. She moaned with pleasure, and began moving her own hand up and down his shaft, feeling its throbbing heat. For several moments Joe's fingers teased, probed, stroked, and massaged until Lily was squirming in uncontrollable desire.

"Let's get in the bed," she pleaded. "I thought I would never see you again. Now, I want to feel you in me, to be sure that it's really you, and this isn't just a dream."

Joe lay her on the bed, then got on top of her. She guided him into the accommodating damp folds of flesh that hid the center of her womanhood. It was well lubricated with the copious flowings of her desire, and when Lily put her hands around behind his butt and pulled forward, he slipped in easily as she writhed in ecstasy beneath him. When he put his mouth to her throat, he could feel her neck muscles twitching. He opened his mouth to suck on the creamy white flesh as she continued to raise her hips wildly to meet his every thrust.

Lily's gasps and moans rose in intensity, and Joe could tell by the increase in her movements and the spasmodic action of her hips that she was nearing orgasm. He rode with her, and when she peaked, her contractions sucked the juices from deep within Joe's body. It was a total, all consuming orgasm, and for an instant he felt keenly with every inch of his body that was in contact with Lily's naked skin.

Afterward, they lay together until their breathing quieted. Then Lily raised up on one elbow and looked down at him.

"I didn't think I'd ever see you again," she said. "I didn't think you would ever come back."

"I didn't think so either," Joe admitted.

"Why did you?"

"Is what we just did a good enough reason?" Joe asked with a smile.

Lily returned the smile. "I don't believe that was why . . . not for a minute. But I'm going to pretend that was why."

16

"JOE! JOE, WAKE UP!" LILY SAID, SHAKING JOE INSIS-tently the next morning.

Joe sat up in bed, then reached for his gun. "What is it?" he asked.

"No, there's no danger!" Lily said quickly. "It's just that I told Claire you were here. She wants to talk to you. She says it's very important."

Joe swung his legs over the edge of the bed, then sat there, naked, as he stretched. "All right," he said. "Send her in."

Lily shook her head. "No," she said.

"What do you mean, no?"

"Not until you put on some clothes. You belong to me, Joe Coulter. At least for this morning. And I'll not have any other woman seeing you like that."

Joe chuckled, then reached for his trousers. "All right," he said. "I'll put my pants on . . . then you can send her in."

When Claire came into the room a moment later, she had a smile that stretched almost from ear to ear. "Joe, am I glad to see you," she said. "And when you hear what I have to say, you are going to be even more glad to see me.''

''Damned if you don't look like the cat that got the bird,'' Joe said.

''Come down to my room with me, Joe. I have something I want to show you.''

Joe looked puzzled. ''What is it?''

''Don't ask questions, just come with me. You'll see,'' Claire said mysteriously.

Pulling on his boots, Joe followed Claire down the hall to her room. He waited as she opened the door, then when she stepped back and invited him in with a sweep of her arm, he stepped inside.

''Hello, Little Brother,'' Win said.

''Win! You're alive!''

Win chuckled. ''Yes. At least, that's what they tell me.''

''But I thought . . .'' Joe stammered.

''That's what Doc wanted people to think,'' Win said.

''I tried to get to you in time to let you know the truth,'' Claire said. ''But you were already gone.''

''Yeah,'' Joe said. ''Well, I had a little business to take care of, then I thought it might be wise to leave town.''

''I heard about the business you took care of,'' Win said. ''Now, let me ask you a question. What are you doing back in town?''

''The truth? I figured I wasn't going to let Pendrake make me run. It seemed like I was, somehow, turning my back on you. I don't know how to explain it, but that's what it seemed like to me.''

''Whatever it is that brought you back, I'm glad to see you here,'' Win said.

''So, what's our first move?''

''Our first move is to make you the sheriff,'' Win said.

''What!'' Joe gasped. He shook his head. ''Hell no, there ain't nobody goin' to pin a badge on me.''

''We've got to.''

''Why do we got to?''

''Because you killed The Albino,'' Win explained. ''If you are a private citizen, Pendrake could perhaps make a case for murder that would stand up, even outside Belle Springs. But if you are a sheriff, it could be explained by saying that The Albino was killed when he resisted arrest.''

"The son of a bitch didn't resist anything," Joe said. "I just went in there and blew his head off, pure and simple.''

Win sighed. "Joe, we're not trying the case here. All we're doing is muddying up the issue a little. This way, you have as much authority as Pendrake. More, if you figure that if it ever actually came to a trial, the town would support you.''

"That's true, Joe," Claire said.

"But you have to have some justification, and a badge will be that justification.''

"Except I won't be legal. The town council that would appoint me isn't even legal.''

"Do you think Pendrake's position is legal?''

"No.''

"Then your claim to be sheriff would be as legal, and would have as much authority, as Pendrake's claim. A court, an honest court, would have to hear both sides. And I don't really think that Pendrake is ready to take his side to an honest court.''

Joe smiled. "I guess you have a point," he said.

"You're damn right I have a point. Claire, how about getting our town council called together again?" Win suggested. "I think it's time the town met their new sheriff. And while we are at it, I'll let them know that I'm still alive.''

AT THAT SAME MOMENT, DOWN THE STREET FROM THE Desert Flower, the door to Ling Lee's laundry opened. Lee, who was hard at work, didn't bother to look up from his ironing board.

"You have laundee for me to do, leave in basket," he called. "You have laundee pick up, I be with you in one minute.''

"It ain't laundry we're here for, you yella-skinned bastared.''

Ling Lee felt a quick surge of fear bolt through him as

he saw Deputies Wallace and Cummins stepping through the front door.

"What you want?" Ling Lee asked.

Wallace shut the front door and locked it, then he pulled down the shade and turned the OPEN—CLOSED sign around, to indicate that the laundry was closed.

"What you do? No can close now," Ling Lee said. "Have people who need laundee."

"Oh, yeah, you can close now, Chinaman. And you're going to stay closed until you pay what you owe."

"I owe nothing."

"You owe the sheriff his tax."

Ling Lee shook his head. "No. We have meeting, we take vote, we say, 'No more do we pay sheriff tax.' "

"We know all about that meeting," Cummins said. "But the Coulter boys were there for that meeting, weren't they? They were the ones who gave you the courage to say that. Well, I have news for you, Chinaman. The Coulters are gone now, both of them. One of them is dead, and the other has hightailed it out of here after committing murder. I don't think you can count on them for help anymore."

"Not count on them," Ling Lee said. "Count on each other."

"Is that a fact? Now, let me see how this works. The idea is that, if nobody pays, then none of you will have to, right?"

"Yes."

"Wrong," Cummins said. "Anyone who doesn't pay will answer to us. And, Chinaman, right now that's you. Are you going to pay the sheriff his rightful taxes, or not?"

"I not pay," Ling Lee said resolutely.

"You think the others will come help you?" Wallace asked. He laughed. "Nobody is going to turn their hand to help a Chinaman. So you may as well pay."

"I not pay," Ling Lee said again.

"Then I guess we're just going to have to make an example out of you," Cummins said. "We need to show the others in this town what will happen to them if they are as foolish as you are."

• • •

JOE, RANDOL, CLAIRE, HARRY, SEMMES, AND JACKSON
were sitting around a table at the Desert Flower. By a special act, "Mayor" Randol had just appointed Joe as the
"Provisional Sheriff" of Belle Springs.

"What does provisional mean?" Joe asked as he pinned
the star onto his shirt.

"It means that you are the sheriff, provided we can get
our claim recognized in the capital. If we can, you will be
the sheriff in fact."

Joe chuckled. "Well, I ain't never been any kind of a
sheriff, provisional or otherwise." He polished the star with
the back of his hand, then looked across the table at the
others. "How does it look?" he asked.

"I think it fits you, Joe," Harry said. "You ask me, you
were born to be a sheriff."

"That right?" Joe pulled his shirt out and looked at the
star. He laughed again. "I'll tell you this. There are more
than just a few folks back in Missouri who would be very
surprised to hear that."

"So," Randol asked, "how are we doing with the tax
repeal? Has anyone encountered any kind of trouble with
Pendrake or any of his deputies?"

"So far, so good," Jackson said. "I haven't taken any
tax money over to Pendrake's office, and I haven't heard
from him."

Semmes pulled a cigar from his inner jacket pocket, bit
the end from it, then bent down to light it over the lantern
that sat in the middle of the table. He took several puffs
before he commented.

"I haven't heard anything from him either, but I don't
expect Pendrake to roll over and play dead," he said. "I
figure he's still trying to come up with some way to handle
it. He had too good of a deal going here, and he isn't just
going to walk away from it. I believe he's going to try
something."

"Let him try," Harry said. "We're ready for him. Especially now that we have our own sheriff."

Suddenly they heard someone shouting outside, and then

the rapid footfalls of someone running down the board side-walk.

"They hung him! They hung him!" someone was shouting outside. "The sheriff and his deputies hung Ling Lee!"

"What?" Harry said. He started toward the door with the others just behind him, then he yelled at the messenger. "What are you saying?"

"The sheriff and his deputies!" the man called back. "They went into Ling Lee's laundry and hauled him out, then carried him down to the hangin' tree. He's down there right now!"

Joe was the first one outside, and he ran down the full length of the street until he came to the hanging tree. There, hanging from the outstretched limb, was Ling Lee. His wife and child were standing nearby looking up at him, and though they weren't crying aloud, Joe didn't think he had ever seen faces with more pain.

"Son of a bitch!" Jackson swore, arriving then. "The bastard did do it!"

"Oh, Harry!" Claire gasped. She turned away from the twisted neck and grimacing features of the Chinese man who had been a part of the town for as long as Claire had been here.

Attached to Ling Lee's shoe was a sign.

Ling Lee
Nothing is as sure as death and taxes.
Ling Lee give up on the taxes. So now
he is dead.

17

As Luscomb cut Ling Lee's body down, Pendrake climbed up onto the back of the buckboard to address the people who had been drawn to the scene.

"I want you folks to take a good look over there," he said, pointing toward the front of the jail. In addition to Wallace, Cummins, and Logan, who were the only three remaining from Pendrake's original force of deputies, there were three more dangerous-looking men.

"Who are those men?" Randol asked.

"They are my new deputies. As you have noted in your newspaper, my force has been cut down something considerable from what it was when I started. So I sent for some more good men. Three of them arrived this morning, another three will be here by noon today."

"Pendrake, you have no authority to hire any more deputies. In fact, you no longer have any authority of any kind, because as the new mayor of this town, I am hereby publicly dismissing you," Randol said.

Pendrake looked at Randol with a strange expression on his face.

"I beg your pardon? As the new mayor? What are you talking about?"

"You may not be aware of it, but the citizens of this town have reorganized and constituted a new city government. We have a new city council and a new mayor. And as the new mayor, I am now telling you that your services are no longer needed."

Several of the townspeople who were gathered around the hanging tree were now hearing, for the first time, of the action of the merchants' meetings. They made their approval known by applauding.

Pendrake pulled his pistol and fired two shots into the air.

"Hold it! Everyone be quiet!" he shouted. As he was shouting, he was also signaling for his deputies to come up beside him. They responded quickly to Pendrake's call and gathered in a semicircle around him, with pistols drawn. They glared menacingly at the crowd.

"Now, hear these words," Pendrake said. "I am going to give you merchants until nine o'clock tomorrow morning to bring me all the money that you owe. That means all the taxes you have held back, plus a fine."

"A fine?" someone asked.

"Yes, a fine, equal to the amount of tax that you already owe me. That means, by nine tomorrow morning, you will have to pay double. Have the money ready, or you will wind up like the Chinaman, hanging from this tree."

"You can't hang all of us!" someone shouted from the back of the crowd.

"That may be," Pendrake agreed. "But I figure that won't make much difference to the ones we do hang. Now, you people go on back to your stores and shops and start doin' some business." He chortled mockingly. "After all, if you are going to pay me tomorrow, you are going to have to make some money."

ONCE AGAIN, THE ROOM AT THE BACK OF THE DESERT Flower was utilized as a meeting place for the new town council. As the various council members arrived for the meeting, their faces reflected obvious signs of worry over the latest turn of events. Even the most nervous, however, agreed that the point of no return had been reached.

"We've come this far," Semmes said. "We can't turn back now. Something has to be done."

"I agree with you, Semmes," Beale said. "But it might be a good idea to pay the taxes tomorrow anyway."

"What? Now, why would you say a damn fool thing like that?" Jackson asked.

"To buy us a little time," Beale replied. "Just until we figure out what to do."

"Beale might be right," Dunnigan suggested. "I mean about buying time. At least, until we come up with a plan."

"We've got a plan," Win said, suddenly appearing in the doorway.

"My God!"

"Where did you—"

"It can't be!"

In addition to the exclamations of surprise, there was a collective gasp from all present, for until this very moment everyone except Joe, Claire, Doc Boyer, and Parker Luscomb had thought that Win was dead.

Joe was with his brother and wearing a badge. This too was a surprise to most of those present.

"Somebody want to explain what's going on here?" Beale asked. He looked at Win. "You ain't a ghost, are you?"

"I'm not a ghost," Win answered.

Doc Boyer stood up. "Clem is right, somebody should explain what's going on, and I reckon that someone is me. I lied when I said that Win Coulter was dead. I lied, and Mr. Luscomb backed me up. I needed the time to tend to his wounds, and I figured the only way I would get it would be for everyone—especially Pendrake and his deputies—to believe that he really was dead."

"Well, by God, I for one am glad you aren't dead!" Semmes said, and his sentiment was seconded by several others.

"Win, you said you have a plan?" Randol asked, trying to get the meeting back on track.

"Yes," Win replied. "I believe that I do. However, it will take the cooperation of the entire town. Everyone must be involved . . . everyone must do their part."

"You can count on us, Mr. Coulter," Dunnigan said.

"Yes, you can count on us," several others stated as well.

"Put the plan into operation, Win," Randol said. "You'll have all the cooperation you need."

"Good, good," Win said. He handed a piece of paper to Randol. "I'd like you to print this in your newspaper today."

Randol looked at the paper, then read aloud: "Fifty thousand dollars in new greenbacks to be transferred from the Citizens Bank in Commerce to the First Bank of Middleton. Specie is to be transferred by courier on the seventeenth, instant."

"Put that right in the middle of the first page," Win said. He smiled. "When Pendrake sees that, he's going to go there like flies to honey."

"That'll get the son of a bitch out of town!" Jackson said. Then quickly he apologized to the ladies for his language.

"It will get him out of town," Randol said. "But I don't know if I want to print that."

"Why not?"

"Yes, we would get Pendrake out of our hair . . . but what about the poor courier who is transporting the money?" Randol shook his head and attempted to hand the note back. "I'm sorry, Mr. Coulter, I wouldn't want it on my conscience if anything happened to the courier."

Win chuckled. "In the first place, there won't be a courier, because there isn't really any money," Win said. "And in the second place, the only one who might be put in danger would be me, because the most logical place to intercept a courier would be at Sandstone Pass. And that's where I intend to be."

"In other words, you're setting yourself up for bait?" Randol asked.

"If you want to catch a fox, you have to bait the trap," Win replied.

"Are you sure you're up for it?" Jackson asked. "I mean, you might not be dead, but you do have a hole in your chest."

"It's a little sore," Win admitted. "But Doc tells me that the danger of havin' the wound mortify on me has passed. I can handle it."

"All right, so we get Pendrake out of town. Then what?"

"I'll take care of Pendrake," Win said.

"You can't handle Pendrake and all his deputies alone. You'll need someone to go with you."

"No, I don't think so. I suspect Pendrake will either be alone, or if anything, no more than one of his deputies will be with him when he shows up. You see, that's a lot of money, and I don't think he will be inclined to split it any more than two ways. That's goin' to leave a few deputies in town."

"And taking care of the deputies who are left behind will be our job," Joe said, standing up, speaking for the first time since the meeting started.

"Our job? You mean you will be here with us?"

"I'm your sheriff, aren't I?" Joe said. Although his question was rhetorical, it received more than a dozen affirmative replies.

"Once we get rid of Pendrake and his deputies," Joe continued, "we'll take over the jailhouse and install our new government."

"I'll be damned!" Jackson said.

"What is it?"

"This really is going to be a revolution, isn't it? I mean a full-scale, all-out, military revolution."

"WALLACE," PENDRAKE SAID THAT AFTERNOON, AS HE read the paper. "Have you seen this?" He handed the paper over to the man who was now his chief of deputies.

"What is it? A story about how mean we are for hangin' the Chinaman?" Wallace asked with a laugh.

"That's not the story I'm interested in," Pendrake said.

He pointed to the page. "This is the one I'm interested in."

Wallace glanced at it, then, perking up at the numbers, read the entire article.

"There's a courier transporting fifty thousand dollars?" he said. He whistled softly. "I didn't know there was that much money in the world."

"It's a lot of money, all right," Pendrake agreed. "Too much to let pass by."

"Are you thinkin' on takin' it?" Wallace asked.

"Hell yes, I'm going to take it. I didn't show you this just to be making conversation," Pendrake replied.

"Fifty thousand dollars!" Wallace said. "Wait until I tell the boys!"

Pendrake shook his head. "We aren't goin' to tell the others anything," he said.

"Why not? I thought you said we were going to take it."

"We are." Pendrake smiled. "But I don't plan on splittin' it more'n two ways."

"You talkin' 'bout just the two of us doin' it?"

"Why not? There's two of us, and only one courier," Pendrake said. "That breaks down to twenty-five thousand dollars for each of us."

Wallace whistled softly. "I wonder how much money it takes for a man to be rich?"

"I don't know," Pendrake answered. "But I can tell you this. Five minutes with that courier, and we're going to be a hell of a lot closer to rich than we are now."

"Tomorrow is when we're supposed to collect the tax. What if we ain't back in time?"

"We ain't comin' back."

"We ain't?"

"Think about it," Pendrake said. "With all the money we'll have, we can go anywhere we want and forget about this place. Who needs a couple hundred dollars tax money."

"Yeah, you're right."

"If Cummins and the others are smart enough to collect it without us . . . they can have it," Pendrake said.

• • •

BECAUSE HIS HARDWARE STORE WAS RIGHT ACROSS THE street from the sheriff's office, and from the Gilded Cage saloon, Arnold Jackson was detailed to see whether or not Pendrake took the bait that had been planted in the newspaper. The next morning, he saw Pendrake and Wallace ride out just before six A.M., headed in the direction of Sandstone Pass. He knew then that their plan was working.

He hurried down to the Desert Flower to give Joe the news.

"All right," Joe said. "This is what we've been waiting for." Joe looked over at Claire. "Claire, you know any of the girls who work at the Gilded Cage?"

"Yes, I know all of them."

"All right, find some way to get them all out of the saloon this morning. When the ball opens, I don't want any of them getting hurt."

"I'll get them out."

"Why don't you let me do it?" Lily asked.

Claire had not heard Lily come down the stairs. "Lily, what are you doing up so early?" she asked.

"I thought I might be able to help in some way, and this is how I can. I should be the one who gets the girls out. Everyone knows that you are part of the council. But I am just an employee here. It wouldn't be that unusual for you to fire me. That would give me a way to go into the Gilded Cage without arousing suspicion."

"She's right, Claire," Jackson agreed.

Claire nodded. "All right, Lily. You get the girls out of there. But be careful."

"I will be."

"Now," Joe said, "our next job is to make sure that all the deputies are in the saloon by eight o'clock. Anybody have any ideas how we can do that?"

"What if we make a sign and post it that says, 'All deputies meet in saloon at eight o'clock'?" Harry suggested.

Dunnigan laughed. "It would be nice if it was that simple."

"Yeah," Semmes said, laughing as well.

"No, wait a minute," Deneke said. "I think it might work at that. I mean, most of the deputies are so new they probably won't even question it."

"He may be right, Joe," Randol said. "Assuming the stupid bastards can read."

"All right, we'll try it," Joe agreed. "Who are we going to get to put the sign up? If one of us does it, and he's seen doing it, they'll know something is wrong."

"What if we got one of the girls from the Gilded Cage to do it?" Lily suggested. "She could say Pendrake gave her the sign."

Joe ran his hand through his hair as he thought about the suggestion. "I wish Win was here," he said. "He's a lot smarter at this kind of thing than I am. He'd know what to do."

"Joe, we have to get the deputies in there by eight," Harry said. "I think Lily's suggestion about using one of the girls from the Gilded Cage makes sense. At any rate, time's getting away from us and that's the best we can do for now."

Finally Joe nodded. "All right. When you get the girls out of there, pick one of them to put up the sign for us."

"What about the customers who might go into the Gilded Cage this morning?" Claire said.

"What about them?"

"Well, not all of them are bad people," Claire explained. "Some of them are also our customers. Is there some way we can warn them, without letting the deputies know what's going on?"

Suddenly Joe snapped his fingers. "I know," he said. "When we make up that sign, have it say that, due to a meeting of all his deputies, the saloon will be closed to the public today."

"Damn good idea," Harry said. "I sure don't know why they call you the dumb one."

"What?" Joe asked. Then, when he realized that his friend was teasing, he laughed out loud.

"All right," Randol said. "We've all got jobs to do. Let's get them done."

18

IT WAS SEVEN O'CLOCK IN THE MORNING, AND DEPUTY Cummins was still asleep in his room at the Gilded Cage when one of the girls knocked on his door and began calling quietly for Sara Ann, the girl who had spent the night in Cummins's bed. Sara Ann was now lying beside him, snoring softly. Though she was the one being called, Cummins was the one who was awakened.

"What is it?" he called irritably. "Who's out there?"

"It's me, Deputy Cummins. Lily Bird."

"Lily Bird? Thought you were workin' at the Desert Flower."

"I was, but I quit. I want to work down here now."

"Yeah? Will you be here tonight?"

"I hope to be," Lily answered.

Cummins had never been with Lily Bird, but the thought of spending the night with her filled him with a pleasant anticipation.

"Deputy Cummins, is Sara Ann with you?"

"What? Yeah, she's with me. Why?"

"I need to see her. It's important. Would you send her out, please?"

"Yeah, you can have her," Cummins grumbled. He pushed on Sara Ann's shoulder.

"Get up!" Cummins said gruffly.

Sara Ann woke up. "What is it?" she asked groggily. "What do you want?"

"I don't want a damn thing," Cummins replied. "But someone out in the hall wants you."

"What do they want me for?"

"How the hell do I know? Get up and go out there and see."

"Uhmm, and I was sleepin' so good too."

"You was snorin' like a hog," Cummins growled. "Now get on out there and see what she wants. That way, maybe I can get a little rest."

"Do you want me to come back, honey?"

"No, I *don't want you to come back, honey*," Cummins said, mimicking her voice. Cummins didn't mind having a woman spend the night with him, but come morning, he would just as soon they be gone. As far as he was concerned, Lily Bird's knock on the door was a fortuitous event.

Sara Ann slipped into her clothes quickly, then stepped out of the room. Cummins heard them whispering outside, and he put the pillow over his head to block them out. Whatever they had to say couldn't possibly be important enough to interrupt his sleep.

Cummins did manage to go back to sleep, though it didn't last long. A short while later there was another loud, impatient knocking on the door, followed by a man's gruff voice.

"Cummins! Cummins, you asleep?"

"Who the hell can sleep with all this bangin' and yellin'?" Cummins replied irritably.

Cummins got out of bed and walked over to the door. When he jerked it open, he saw Deputy Logan standing there.

"Dammit all to hell, Logan, what's goin' on around here this mornin'?" Cummins asked. "First that damn woman wakes me up, and now you. What do you want?"

"Pendrake has called a meeting for ever'body at eight-thirty. It's pert' near that now."

"A meetin'? What for? We don't need no meetin'. If the people don't pay their taxes, we know what to do."

"I don't know what it's about," Logan said. "But it must be important. I've never known him to call any meetings before. He wants ever'one to be downstairs."

Cummins ran a hand through his tousled hair, then scratched his chin. "All right," he said. "All right, tell 'im to hold his horses. I'll be down in a few minutes."

Cummins poured some water from the pitcher into the basin and splashed some of it onto his face. Then he got dressed, pulled on his boots, and strapped on his gun.

As Cummins reached for his hat, he happened to look out through the window. He saw Semmes and Deneke going into the still-closed hardware store. Seeing two of the local businessmen going into a closed store wasn't, in itself, all that strange. But both were carrying rifles, and that was curious.

He didn't give that much thought, though, as he finished dressing then went downstairs. There, he saw all the deputies sitting around the tables, talking quietly among themselves. Only Logan was there from the original deputies. The other six were men that Pendrake had only recently hired.

The new men sat apart from Logan. Wallace, Cummins, and Logan had not accepted the new deputies with open arms. As far as they were concerned, the new men weren't needed, and their presence just meant there would be more pieces cut from the pie. Pieces that would have otherwise gone to them.

As Cummins thought of Wallace, he realized that he wasn't there. Neither was Pendrake.

"So, where is he?" Cummins asked as he came over to the table where Logan was sitting alone.

"Pendrake, or Wallace?" Logan replied.

"Either one of them. Where are they?"

"Don't know," Logan answered. "Haven't seen either one of them this morning."

"What do you mean, you haven't seen either one of
them? How the hell did you know we were supposed to
have a meetin' if you ain't seen either one of them?"

" 'Cause of the sign that's posted on the door over
there," Logan said.

"Sign on the door?"

Cummins went over to look at the sign Logan had told
him about.

*Notice: I want all deputies to meet in the saloon at
8:30. The saloon will be closed then, and all others
must leave. By order of Harley Pendrake, Sheriff.*

"Ain't never know'd Pendrake to leave no sign before,"
Cummins said. He rubbed his chin, then looked at the group
of new deputies. "Any of you see Pendrake this mornin'?"
he asked.

All shook their heads no.

"What is it, Cummins?" Logan asked, seeing that Cummins was beginning to wonder about things.

"I don't know," Cummins replied. "Something just
seems a little strange to me, that's all. Pendrake calls this
meetin', but he ain't here. There's somethin' . . ." Cummins started to say, but as he couldn't put his finger on
what was bothering him, he was unable to form the words
to express his concern. As a result he let the incomplete
sentence dangle in the air, teasing with its potential.

"What is it, Cummins?" Logan asked, totally unaware
of anything unusual going on.

"Ah, probably nothing," Cummins finally said. "I need
a drink."

"Kind of early in the mornin' for that, ain't it, Cummins?" one of the new deputies asked.

Angrily, Cummins whirled toward the deputy who had
made the comment. He pointed at him. "By God, if I say
I need a drink, who the hell are you to question it?" Cummins asked angrily.

"Didn't mean nothin' by it," the new deputy replied,

throwing his hands up as if to ward Cummins off. "I was just passin' a remark, that's all."

"You pass your goddamn remarks to someone else," Cummins growled. He walked around behind the bar and poured his own liquor, standing there for a moment while he tossed the drink down.

When he finished the drink he slapped the shot glass down on the bar. "All right," he said. "So what the hell is goin' on here? What's this meeting about, and why isn't Pendrake here?"

"Ain't nobody figured that out yet," one of the new deputies said.

"Anybody think to knock on his bedroom door?"

"I already did," Logan replied. "I checked his room and I checked Wallace's room. Ain't neither one of 'em here."

Cummins walked over to the batwing doors and looked out onto the street. To his surprise, he didn't see anyone; not one wagon, horse, or pedestrian. He looked toward Jackson's Hardware Store but saw nothing there either.

"What day is this?" he asked.

"I don't know. September something or the other."

"No, I mean what day of the week? Is this Sunday?"

"No. It's Thursday, I think. Or maybe Friday."

"You sure it ain't Sunday?"

"I'm positive it ain't Sunday. Why do you ask?"

"I don't know," Cummins replied. "It just seems awful quiet for some reason. I mean, have you looked out into the street? There ain't nobody or nothin' out there."

"Wonder where Pendrake is," Logan said.

"Go wake up the girls," Cummins ordered. "Maybe one of them will know where they are."

"Ain't none of the girls here," one of the new deputies answered.

"What do you mean?"

"I seen 'em all leavin' here, 'bout forty-five minutes ago."

"You saw the girls leavin'? All of 'em? Where were they goin'?"

"I don't know, but they seemed damned determined to

get out of here. I figured they just didn't want to be here durin' the meetin'.''

Cummins looked over at Logan. "Look here, Logan, there is somethin' wrong here. Take a look outside."

"Take a look at what?" Logan replied. "You said yourself there wasn't nothin' out there."

"Take a look," Cummins said again. "Tell me if you see anyone."

Logan walked over to the door to look outside. "Just them fellas fixin' the roof up on top of the hardware store."

"Some folks fixin' a roof? Where?"

Logan pointed across the street. "Up there, on the roof of the hardware store. Patchin' it, I guess. Oh, and there's somebody on the roof of the feed store too. What the hell is this, fix your roof day or somethin'?"

Cummins moved quickly to the door and looked up toward the roof. He saw someone running, bent over at the waist.

"Fixin' a roof, my ass. That son of a bitch is carrying a rifle!" Cummins said.

Now it all came together for him.

"Get your guns out, men, we're about to be attacked!"

"What are you talking about, attacked?" one of the new deputies asked. "Who's attacking us? Indians?" He laughed at his joke.

"No, goddamn it! The town is!" Cummins shouted back. "Hell, half the damn town is crawlin' around out there on roofs and behind buildings. And they've all got rifles."

At the same time, Logan saw someone with a rifle looking out of one of the upstairs rooms at the hotel.

"Son of a bitch! Cummins is right!" Logan shouted. He drew his pistol and shot toward the hotel. His bullet punched a hole in the glass window, but other than that, it did no damage.

"What did you shoot for, you dumb bastard?" Cummins shouted.

"What do you mean, why did I shoot? I seen someone at the hotel pointin' a rifle this way."

"As long as they thought they had us in the dark, we had the advantage," Cummins said. "Now they know that we know."

"So what? There ain't nothin' out there but a bunch of ribbon clerks and storekeeps," Logan said derisively. "If you ask me, we ought to just go out there and—unnnh!"

Logan's declaration was cut short by a bullet fired from somewhere across the street. The bullet caught him high in the chest and spun him around. He went down, spewing a little fountain of blood. He looked up with an expression of surprise on his face.

"A ribbon clerk," he said. "Who would've thought . . ." Those were his last words.

"Get these tables turned over, men!" Cummins shouted. "Get 'em up to the windows! We've got a fight on our hands!"

JOE WAS CLIMBING ONTO THE ROOF OF THE HARDWARE store when he heard the shooting start. He was carrying a heavy box and his movement was somewhat restricted. He set the box down and looked around as the other men on the roof, all of whom were armed with rifles, were firing into the saloon across the street.

"What did you start shooting for?" he asked. "I thought we were going to wait for the signal."

"We couldn't help it, Joe," Harry replied. "They must've seen us, 'cause they started the shootin'."

"All right, it doesn't matter," Joe said. He opened the box to reveal several small, hastily made bombs, consisting of empty bean cans filled with blasting powder. Joe picked one of them up.

"All right," he said. "Harry, light the fuse, then step back. I'll throw it."

"Right," Harry said. Harry lit the fuse, and when it was sputtering, Joe stood up and threw it across the street, toward the Gilded Cage. It crashed through one of the windows on the other side.

Joe got down to wait for the blast. He was surprised when, a second later, the bomb, still unexploded, came back out of the saloon. It went off with a roar, in the middle of the street.

"Damn!" Joe said. "I gave them too much time. The fuse was too long."

Joe cut the fuse on the next bomb in half. "Now light it," he said. "We'll try it again."

"Joe, that's much too short. It'll go off in your hand."

"No, it won't. Light it," Joe insisted.

Harry lit the fuse and Joe stood up to throw it. This time the bomb exploded in midair, halfway between the roof of the hardware store and the saloon. The fuse was indeed too short.

"All right," Joe said, picking up another one. "This time we'll get it right."

Once more Joe cut the fuse, though not quite as short as he had cut the previous one. Again the fuse was lit, and again Joe stood up to throw it. The defenders in the saloon concentrated their fire on Joe. Bullets hit the false front wall of the hardware store just in front of him, and whizzed by his ear as they burned the air close to him. None of the bullets found their mark, however, and Joe was able to throw yet a third bomb.

A little stream of smoke marked the path of the missile as it hurtled from the top of the hardware store, across the street, then down toward the front window of the Gilded Cage. It broke out some more of the window as it went inside.

This time the fuse was perfectly cut, for an instant after the bomb broke through the window, there was a deafening blast from within the saloon. Fire, smoke, glass shards from the windows, and splinters of the batwing doors flew out into the street.

Four deputies came outside then, firing as they ran, pointing their pistols at the buildings of the town and shooting randomly. To a man, they were cut down by a hail of gunfire from the citizen militia that had been raised for the occasion.

"Cease fire!" Joe shouted, holding his hand up to get attention. "Cease fire!"

The firing stopped and for a moment there was absolute silence. Then, when the citizens of the town realized that they had won their revolution, they began to cheer.

Doc Boyer was the first one to go down onto the street. There, he began examining the bodies to see if anyone was left alive. The others joined him in the street, laughing and talking about their victory, happy and proud that once again the town belonged to them.

Claire, Lily, Helga, and the other women, as well as the children of the town, had taken shelter in the basement of the hardware store. Now the three women ventured out into the street with the men to see what was going on.

"I'd better check inside," Doc said. "There may be some wounded in there."

"If there are, you may need some help, Doc," Lily said. "I'll go with you."

"Thanks," Doc said.

Shortly after they went inside, there was a muffled shot. Startled, Joe and the others looked toward the bomb-damaged front of the saloon. A moment later, they could see Doc coming through the wreckage. He had a strange expression on his face, and it took only a moment to see why.

Doc was walking at the point of a gun. He was being held hostage.

"All right!" Cummins said, waving his pistol around. He had the advantage over the citizens of the town, not only because he was holding Doc Boyer hostage, but also because he had a loaded pistol, whereas the small citizens' army had been equipped with rifles, most of which were now left behind them.

"I want a horse!" Cummins shouted. "I want a horse, and I want five hundred dollars in greenbacks! If I don't have it in one minute, Doc dies."

"You realize, don't you, that if you kill him, you won't have any hold over us?" Joe cautioned him.

"I don't give a damn!" Cummins shouted. "Do you understand me? I don't give a damn! I already killed the whore who came in with him, for setting us up this morning. If I kill one more of you bastards before you kill me, I can die a happy man. Now get me a horse and that money." Cummins smiled an evil smile. "You folks been wantin' to get rid of me, here's your chance."

At the news of Lily's death, Joe was ready to leap at the devil, but suddenly the flat, popping sound of a single rifle shot echoed from the adjacent buildings. A bullet hole appeared in Cummins's forehead and he fell back into the street, his head landing in a pile of horse manure.

"What the hell?" Deneke asked. "Who fired that shot?"

"*Ja*, I fired the shot," Helga said, stepping out through the front door of her cafe. From the end of the barrel of the rifle she was holding, there arose a small, curling stream of smoke.

"*You* killed him, Helga?" Joe asked. He smiled. "Well, I didn't know you had it in you, but I'm glad you did."

Helga walked over to the body then stood there, looking down at it. She spit on Cummins's body. "Three months ago this man raped me," she said.

"This son of a bitch raped you?" Dunnigan asked, surprised by the announcement. "Why, Helga, you should have told someone."

"And who would I tell?" Helga asked. "The sheriff? Maybe if I tell the sheriff, he might do it too. No, there was no one to help, so I keep my shame to mine own self."

Dunnigan nodded in agreement. "I reckon you've got a point there," he said.

"I tell him then, that someday I will kill him. He laugh at me then," Helga said. She stared for a long moment at Cummins's still form. "I do not think he laugh now."

19

WIN WAS AWARE THAT THE TWO MEN WERE FOLLOWING him, riding parallel with him. He also knew when they left him, to ride ahead in order to get into position to set up the ambush.

The ambush point would be just ahead, where the trail squeezed down to a narrow path going through a needlelike draw. Recalling his days with Quantrill, he knew that this was an ideal place to set up an ambush, for at the other end of the draw a real courier would be a sitting duck.

When Win reached the draw he knew that for the next several seconds he would be out of the line of sight of those who were waiting for him. This was where he would make his move. As he passed under a large rock outcropping, he stood in his saddle, found a good handgrip, then pulled himself up into the rocks. Once in the rocks, he was able to climb over the top of the pass while his horse continued on through.

Win ran at a crouch to the far end of the pass. From there, he could hear the slow, measured clop of his horse's hooves echoing through the long, narrow canyon. He pulled his pistol and waited . . . just as he knew that Pendrake and Wallace were doing.

The sound of the hoofbeats came closer until they were almost upon him.

"Now!" Win heard Pendrake shout, and the narrow chasm was filled with the sound of exploding gunshots and whistling bullets.

Win's riderless horse bolted out of the canyon.

"What the hell? Where is he?" Wallace asked.

"We must've got 'im! Grab the horse!" Pendrake ordered. "The money will be in the saddlebags!"

Wallace stepped in front of the horse and threw his arms up. The horse slid to a stop, its iron hooves striking sparks on the rocky ground. Wallace grabbed the halter and began to calm the horse.

"You hold him," Pendrake said, starting toward the saddlebags. "I'll get the money."

"There isn't any money," Win said, suddenly standing up.

"What the hell? It's Coulter!" Wallace shouted. "But how can that be? I thought The Albino killed you!"

"He did kill me," Win said. "But I've come back from hell to get you."

"What? You're a ghost?"

"He ain't no ghost," Pendrake said. "Ghosts don't need guns."

"Drop your guns and put up your hands," Win ordered.

Pendrake and Wallace did as they were ordered. "We ain't fightin' you, Coulter. You can't shoot us! We ain't fightin' you!"

WIN BOUND PENDRAKE AND WALLACE HAND AND FOOT IN their saddles for the ride back to Belle Springs.

"Would you answer a question for me?" Pendrake asked. "The whole town turned out for your funeral. If that wasn't you in the box, who was it?"

"It wasn't anyone. Just a few rocks to give it weight."

"Was the whole town in on it?"

"Nope. Just a few."

Pendrake laughed dryly. "I got to hand it to you, Coulter. That's one of the slickest tricks I ever heard, makin' the whole town think you was dead like that. You put one over on us. Now, I'll be interested to see how you handle it when you get us back to my town. You don't really think my deputies are going to let you put me in jail, do you?"

"When they learn that you had planned to steal the money and leave them high and dry, I think they might."

Pendrake chuckled. "You think they'll believe you? Not for a minute. If you're smart, you'll just ride off now. Otherwise, you'll be the one spendin' the night in jail. And I'm tellin' you now . . . come mornin', I'll hang you."

"We'll just see who gets hanged, and who does the hangin'," Win said.

IT WASN'T YET LATE AFTERNOON WHEN WIN LED HIS TWO prisoners back into Belle Springs. There were people on the street, more people than he had ever seen on the streets before.

"What is this?" Pendrake asked. "What's goin' on? Somethin' seems different."

Win saw at once what was different. The people of Belle Springs, who were normally reticent and withdrawn, were now laughing and animated. As he passed by Jackson's Hardware Store he saw why. There, in the front window, not in coffins but tied to boards, were the bodies of eight deputies.

"Pendrake, my God, look in the window of the hardware store!" Wallace shouted in alarm. "They're dead, all of 'em!"

Win looked toward Pendrake and saw the facade of bravado fall away. It wasn't until that very moment that Pendrake realized he was truly the captive and not the captor.

When Win stopped in front of the sheriff's office, he was met by his brother and several of the town's citizens.

"Well, Little Brother, looks like your plan worked," Win said as he swung down from the saddle.

"I'll say it did," Dunnigan replied. He saw the two sullen men tied in the saddle. "And with them two, we can now make a clean sweep of it."

"So what are we going to do with them?" Deneke asked.

"What do you mean, what are we goin' to do?" Win replied. "We're goin' to hang 'em."

"We can't do that," Deneke said.

"Why not?"

"It wouldn't be legal. I mean, we took our town from these people in the first place because of their lawlessness. I don't want us to become just as lawless, and hanging them without a trial would be nothing more than a lynching."

"Well, hell, give the bastards a trial. Then hang 'em," Win suggested.

"We don't have a judge here. How are we going to do that?"

"Wait a minute, Bob," Randol said. "You know, we do have some precedence here. I think we could hang them, and make it legal."

"How?"

"We had a revolution, right? An armed revolution?"

"Yes."

"That puts us under martial law. And, as we are subject to martial law, we, the Belle Springs militia, can convene a court, select a jury, and appoint a prosecutor and counselor for the defense."

Pendrake's face went gray. "You can't do that," he said. "You got no right to do that."

"What are you bitching about, Pendrake? At least you are going to get a trial. That's more of a chance than you ever gave anyone."

"Whatever you do here won't stand up in a real court, and you know it!" Pendrake said.

"I'm the mayor now. I will take it upon myself to convene the court. If there are any questions with the legitimate authorities later on, I will be solely responsible for my actions, and I will take my case all the way to the Supreme Court, if necessary."

"You're saying you would take this case to the Supreme Court?" Pendrake asked.

"I'll take it there if I have to," Randol said with a cold smile. "But trust me, it won't matter to the two of you. You'll both be long dead by then."

THOUGH THE TRIAL BEGAN LESS THAN AN HOUR LATER, the entire town had gotten word of it so that nearly everyone was squeezed into the empty hardware store to watch. The fact that the eight bodies had not been removed and were still standing their ghostly watch from the front window added a touch of the macabre to the proceedings.

Jackson had been appointed prosecutor, and he opened the argument by charging Pendrake with terrorizing a town and murdering the four cowboys by their mock trial and illegal hanging. He chose that incident, rather than the hanging of Ling Lee, because no one actually saw Ling Lee until after he was already hanged. On the other hand, almost the entire town was present for the hanging of the four cowboys.

Jackson interviewed several witnesses, all of whom told how they had watched while the young cowboys were placed on the back of a buckboard wagon with ropes around their necks, and how the buckboard team was caused to dash forward, jerking the buckboard from under the young cowboys' feet, causing them to be hanged. Telling the details of the hanging to the judge and jury was an exercise in redundancy since the judge and every member of the jury had also witnessed it.

Harry Conners had been appointed as the defense attorney, and as soon as Jackson sat down, he cross-examined the witnesses.

"Mr. Semmes, when the cowboys were hanged, was it by a large, unruly mob?"

"Well, there were a lot of people there."

"Was the crowd unruly? Did its members participate in the hanging?"

"No. Only the sheriff and his deputies participated."

"Were the sheriff and his deputies wild and unruly?"

Semmes looked over at Pendrake. "No," he said. "They were cold and calculating."

"Have you ever been the witness to a legal hanging?"
Harry asked.

"Yes. I seen me a hangin' in San Antonio."

"A legal hanging?"

"Oh, yes, it was legal, all right."

"How would you describe it? The legal hanging, I mean.
Was it wild and unruly? Or cold and calculating?"

"Well, I guess you could call it cold and calculating,"
Semmes replied, realizing that he was using the same words
of description.

"Then, in your mind, the only thing that was different
about this hanging from the one in San Antonio is that you
don't believe this one was legal?"

"I know this one wasn't legal."

"But it was prescribed by the court, wasn't it?"

"By Pendrake's court."

"But it was a court, not a mob lynching."

"I suppose you could call it that."

"Thank you. No further questions."

As Pendrake and Wallace both refused to testify in their
own behalf, the court was then over, except for the sum-
mation. Harry stood up and faced the jury that had been
selected from among the townspeople.

"Gentlemen of the jury, the defendants, Harley Pendrake
and Larry Wallace, are not the kind of men you would want
as neighbors, or friends, and certainly not as your enemy.
They are men who have lived for many years by their guns,
and there is no doubt in my mind that they have killed
many men. But we are not trying them for living by their
guns, nor for killing many men. We are bringing them to
trial on a very specific charge, for the murder, by hanging,
of the four young cowboys about whom we have already
spoken.

"If that is all we can find to try them on, then I've got
some bad news for you. You can't find them guilty. All
you have to do is recall the testimony of Mr. Semmes to
see that it wasn't murder. It was a court-ordered execution.

"But, what court, you may ask. I will answer you. It is
the same court we are in now, gentlemen, for according to

Mr. Jackson, the prosecutor in this case, the very legality of what we are doing now is based upon the establishment of a court in this town by Sheriff Harley Pendrake. We cannot find his court illegal for him, and legal for ourselves. We can't have it both ways.'' Harry looked over at Pendrake and Wallace, who were now smiling smugly. ''These two men are guilty of a lot of things . . . but they aren't guilty of the charges that have been filed against them today.''

The townspeople, who had thought that perhaps Harry Conners would mount a listless defense, now sat stunned by the effectiveness of his argument. Jackson sat at the prosecutor's table for a full moment, marshaling his thoughts, before he stood up and walked over to address the jury.

''Gentlemen of the jury,'' he said. ''Harry Conners has, indeed, given us something to consider. He has said that we cannot find Pendrake's court illegal without finding ourselves illegal for using the same court. And there is merit to his argument, for, in the final analysis, we must be certain that what we are doing is not only legally, but morally right.

''Can we use this court to try Harley Pendrake and Larry Wallace? And if this court finds them guilty and sentences them to death by hanging, can we carry out that terrible sentence without permanent damage to our legal status as a civilized community, and to our immortal souls?''

Jackson crossed his arms to study the jury and saw that, to a man, he had their rapt attention.

''The answer to that question is . . . yes. We can act as a court. Because you see, gentlemen, the court itself is not on trial here. What is on trial here is the *perversion* of that court, as was perpetrated by these two men. You can find Pendrake and Wallace guilty of perverting the court to commit the murder of those four young cowboys, while at the same time affirming the legality of the court itself. Therefore, I urge you to return a verdict of guilty.''

Ed Randol, now acting as judge of the court, turned to the jury. ''The jury may now retire to deliberate,'' he said.

While the jury was in deliberation, Win, Joe, Claire, Randol, Jackson, and Harry Conners waited.

"I must tell you, Harry, I expected you to roll over. I was quite impressed at the defense you put up for those two men."

"And I am equally impressed by the logic of your prosecution," Harry replied. "Did you study law?"

"I read for it, yes," Jackson replied. "But unless a man lives in a big city with several opportunities to ply his avocation . . . he could starve."

Harry laughed. "I know," he said. "That's why I am a bartender."

"Why, Harry Conners," Claire said, "you mean you also read for the law?"

"Yes," Harry said.

"My. I am very impressed with my new business partner," she said.

"The jury is comin' back!" someone shouted from the rear of the building, and everyone took their seats to await the verdict. When the jury was seated, Randol looked toward Dunnigan, who had been selected as foreman of the jury.

"Has the jury reached a verdict?" Randol asked.

"We have, Your Honor," Dunnigan replied, playing out his role with solemnity.

"How find you?"

"To the charge of terrorizing the town, we find the defendants not guilty." Dunnigan looked out over the townspeople. "We figure we are the guilty ones for lettin' 'em get away with it for so long."

There were several gasps and groans of protest from those in the audience, and Randol, using a carpenter's hammer as a gavel, banged it on the table several times in a call for order.

Pendrake and Wallace smiled smugly.

"How find you as to the second charge?" Randol asked.

"To the charge of murdering the four young cowboys, we find the defendants guilty."

This time the audience erupted into cheers and applause

and, again, Randol had to bang his gavel for quiet. Finally, with the audience silent, Randol cleared his throat.

"Thank you, gentlemen of the jury. You are now dismissed. Would the prisoners please stand?"

Pendrake and Wallace, their beady eyes now reflecting fear, stood.

"Harley Pendrake and Larry Wallace, you have been tried by a court that was established by yourselves, validated by martial law, and presided over by me. This court has found you both guilty of murder in the first degree, and therefore I sentence you both to be hanged by the neck until you are dead. Sentence is to be carried out tomorrow morning. Please escort the prisoners across the street to the jail. This court is adjourned."

As four men stepped up to grab the two prisoners, Pendrake looked over to Win and Joe.

"You two boys come early tomorrow," he said. "You'll get to see us dance."

Win shook his head. "You'll have to do it without us," he said. "We sold our interest in the Desert Flower, and Joe has turned in his badge. We'll be moving on."

"What? You mean you've sold out? You're leaving town?"

"That's right."

Pendrake looked puzzled. "I don't understand," he said. "If you are leaving town, why were you so all fired up to get me? What was in it for you?"

"Nothing," Win replied.

"Then, why did you do it?"

Win smiled. "Some things you do just for the hell of it," he said.